Russia Rising

Seth Chanowitz

Dedication

This novel has emerged after over two years of hard work. I would like to thank my mother and my wife, Veronika, for their assistance and patience in the process of drafting and re-drafting this book. I would also like to thank all those individuals who assisted me while I was working as an intelligence analyst for the United States government. I made many friends and received lots of assistance from co-workers who were employed by many different intelligence agencies, while working very long hours at the Terrorist Threat Integration Center and National Counter Terrorism Center. This book is dedicated to those hard working intelligence professionals, the many individuals and friends I encountered and received assistance from while living in Finland, and members of my family who resided and subsequently left Russia and the former Soviet Union.

Chapter 1

May 2014: Flight of Freedom

Vantaa, Finland

At 4:00 a.m., two cars approach an airport hangar situated in an open field within a densely forested tract of land. The automobiles possess a unique Moose logo on the passenger door, along with the words "Outlandish Public Relations Agency" boldly emblazoned in English.

The cars park near the hangar, which contains an airplane with the word "Freedom" printed prominently on it. Harri Bergstrom, a thin, bearded, blond-haired, blue-eyed man in his mid-thirties, exits his automobile. He wears rimless eyeglasses, a light-colored red shirt, and blue jeans. He is the CEO and founder of Outlandish PR, which is an innovative public relations agency that supports numerous nonviolent actions against governments that abuse human rights. Then, Katya Niemi, a twenty-something, red-haired woman, exits the car parked adjacent to Harri's car. She has spiked red hair, nose and lip piercings, and is wearing a peasant blouse.

"*Hei!*" Katya announces and gives Harri a kiss on the cheek.

"Did you get any sleep last night?" Harri inquires.

"No, I was too nervous about the flight to sleep," Katya says.

"Don't worry. I think the movie on this flight will be nice, in any case." Harri smiles, hoping to diffuse Katya's nervousness.

"I am more worried about how this flight will end. Hopefully, like in the movies, it will have a happy ending," Katya remarks.

"Did you bring all the teddy bears and leaflets we prepared with those messages? I just have to fly this crazy contraption low enough in the most secure airspace in Europe to avoid the Belarus military shooting us out of the sky. The teddy bears and leaflets are your responsibility," Harri says.

"The bears are all here," Katya says.

Katya takes the thirty bags of teddy bears and leaflets from her truck and loads them into the aircraft. Harri engages in an inspection of the airplane. After he appears satisfied with the aircraft's condition, he opens the airplane's door and hops into the pilot seat.

"How is everything going with the bears?" Harri yells.

"Almost completed," Katya responds while standing in front of her car's trunk.

Harri starts the plane's engine, which quickly drowns out all the noise within the cockpit. Katya places the last of the bags of teddy bears behind the two seats of the cockpit.

Harri looks at Katya. "We are either going to be in Warsaw or in jail in several hours. Let's hope we end up in Poland, as jail is not a comfortable place in Belarus," Harri remarks.

"*Joo*," Katya said in typical Finnish style.

Harri turns on the aircraft's radio and speaks into the microphone. "Is everything in place, Jaanika?"

There is silence for a moment. "Yes, I am ready. I'm located near a beautiful park in Minsk. The weather is great here. I will be in communication with you as you travel to your objective. Good luck with your flight."

In Minsk, Belarus, Jaanika Olson, a red-haired, green-eyed, five-foot-four, twenty-something woman from Minneapolis, Minnesota is wearing blue jeans and a dark shirt. Jaanika is an Estonian-American, currently living in Finland and attending the law school at Helsinki University. Harri approached her to assist with the flight, and she volunteered on the spot, as she had known of Harri's involvement promoting human rights globally.

"We will need all the luck we can get. Hope to see you in Poland," Harri remarks.

Harri looks at Katya. "I think it's time. History in the making." He pauses and adds with uncertainty, "Maybe."

The plane starts to roll faster and faster as it gathers momentum, traveling down the small, private runway. Harri directs the plane upward. The wheels lift off the ground, and the plane rises in the air above Finland's capital. Harri and Katya look out the window after several minutes and spy the large white and blue Orthodox Church, which is an iconic landmark, located near Helsinki's harbor below. Many buildings on Finland's small islands, located close to Helsinki's harbor, are soon visible, along with ferries sailing across the Baltic Sea to Swedish, Lithuanian, Russian, and Estonian ports.

"That was easy. Now on to Minsk," Harri announces.

Katya smiles. She remarks, "*Niin.*"

The plane flies over the Baltic Sea and south to the Baltic States. At 5:45 a.m., the plane crosses from Lithuania into Belarus at a very low altitude.

Harri looks at Katya. "Let's hope that the Belarus military was celebrating and drinking all last night. Hopefully, they are still sleeping or hung over."

"I'm counting on it," Katya responds, clearly worried.

It's July fourth, the day following Belarus's National Day. Huge military parades occurred in central Minsk the previous day. All branches of the Belarus military were in attendance to celebrate Belarus and its all-powerful autocratic leader, Alexander Lukashenko. He is the president forever of the small nation that borders Poland, Russia, the Ukraine, and Lithuania. Lukashenko is pro-Russian and has kept the country in a pre-Soviet Union state, which is securely within Russia's orbit. Statues of Lenin, Marx, and Stalin remain in Minsk decades after Communism's collapse. The infamous secret police, known as the KGB, is ruthless and unreformed, and any democratic dissent results in jail, torture, or exile from the country. Harri and his PR agency have embraced the cause of freedom and human rights in Belarus. With this daring flight, Harri hopes to direct the world's attention to the plight of dissidents in Belarus, who are locked away in its gulag-like prison system.

Harri peers below and views a vast expanse of farmland and forests. There are small houses, dilapidated buildings, and dirt roads that populate

Belarus's countryside. Both Katya's and Harri's nerves are on edge.

"We are in the air, Jaanika," Harri announces into the microphone of the cockpit's radio. This is an agreed-upon code to indicate his plane has entered Belarus airspace.

The radio then cuts off for a second. "Sounds good. Hope you are enjoying the flight," Jaanika says.

"Next stop is Minsk and Lukashenko's presidential palace. Do you think we should land and ask for a tour?" Harri says.

"Not if we ever want to see Finland again. Besides, I have an appointment with my stylist in Warsaw and don't want to leave her waiting. President Lukashenko will have to wait for another day to see me." Katya laughs.

The fuel gauge in the cockpit indicates the plane is using more petrol than expected. Harri's expression reveals he is a little worried, but he still feels confident that there will be enough fuel for the flight to succeed.

The plane begins rocking violently. Katya and Harri both look out the window. Katya attempts to steady herself by placing her hand on the cockpit's wall, as items are tossed about throughout the cockpit.

Harri's head smashes on the controls, and a black, swelling bruise appears on his face.

"Ahh!" Harri yells.

"Are you okay? Katya asks with fear in her voice.

"No worse for wear. I can still fly the plane." Harri puts his hand on his head to check for any blood.

"Do you think that was an anti-aircraft missile?" Katya remarks, worried. She then looks at Harri's bruise for a second to see if he is harmed.

"No, we would not be alive if it was a missile. I think turbulence is the likely problem." Harri's unease is apparent.

Harri and Katya look out of the cockpit window but see no sign of any airplanes or any other defenses from the Belarus military. After five minutes, the turbulence subsides, though the nerves of the two are on edge.

The outskirts of the capital city of Minsk emerges below. Farmlands and dirt roads are transformed into wide streets and boulevards.

Katya reaches into the compartment in the back of her seat and busily begins arranging the bags of teddy bears and leaflets in order so that she can easily drop them out of the window situated next to her.

"Is everything in order for the drop? We're approaching central Minsk." Harri looks at Katya.

"*Joo!* Let's do this," Katya retorts and opens the window next to her.

Harri announces on the cockpit's radio, "Bears, bears, bears."

On the Ground in Central Minsk, Belarus

"I can see you. I love you Finns," Jaanika announces into the microphone of her portable radio. On the ground in Gorky Park in central Minsk, Jaanika is intently filming the aircraft with a small video camera.

In the Plane above Minsk

Katya begins dropping the bears and the leaflets out the window. One by one, each teddy bear's parachute opens. Each has a message written in English and Russian attached to the bear stating, "Freedom and Human Rights for Belarus." Each bear is brown, contains a button nose, is furry, and has a small message attached to it. The white parachutes open, and the bears begin to descend and glide gently to the ground. The leaflets also fall from the sky with a message of "Democracy for Belarus" written on them.

On the Ground in Central Minsk

"Those bears look awesome in the sky," Jaanika announces in English on the radio microphone. She watches the small plane buzzing above Minsk and spots hundreds of bears gliding to the ground through the viewfinder of her video camera.

Ordinary Minsk residents who are walking on the street in central Minsk stop in their tracks and are suddenly awestruck at the sight of the teddy bears descending in the sky above Belarus on a beautiful, almost cloudless day in Minsk. The bears' parachutes open, and they begin to drift down to the ground. At first, hundreds of bears appear as white dots that contrast against the sun of the summer day. The bears slowly begin reaching the ground, and the leaflets soon follow.

Jaanika continues videotaping and sees many individuals walking in central Minsk stop in their tracks and look up to the sky. Many take out their smartphones and snap pictures. The local police on the ground are amused and miffed. The bears and leaflets begin landing in downtown Minsk.

Some individuals walking on the street in central Minsk pick up the bears and leaflets and cheer as they read the messages. It's a surreal moment in Belarus. The dictator of Belarus is being attacked by teddy bears with messages of freedom.

In the Plane above Minsk, Belarus

Harri looks at Katya. "Are the bears all gone?"

Katya exclaims, "Yes. Freedom for Belarus! Down with the dictator Lukashenko!"

"Let's head to Poland. On my next trip to Belarus, I will enjoy some of the tourist attractions in Minsk," Harri jokes.

Harri changes the plane's direction. The plane can be seen veering away from Minsk and heads west in the direction of Poland. Both Katya and Harri seem elated.

Harri announces on the radio, "Jaanika, see you in Helsinki! *Hei Hei!*"

At 8:00 a.m., the plane finally crosses the Belarus–Poland border. In the cockpit fifteen minutes later, the engine sputters intermittently. Harri looks worriedly at the fuel gauge, which indicates that the plane is almost empty of petrol. Harri looks at Katya. "I have bad news for you, Katya. My estimates of fuel usage on this flight were incorrect. The turbulence we experienced caused us to use much more fuel than I expected. In other words, we have no more petrol," Harri says.

"Harri, tell me some good news," Katya demands.

"I think we are going to land very soon." Harri smiles but shows an expression of fear.

Harri looks down intently, searching for an open field or runway on the ground in Poland. The plane's engine emits a sputtering sound as the last amounts of fuel are used.

Harri radios to the Polish air control.

"May day. May day. We have to land as we have run out of fuel. This is Freedom 1. We are traveling from Helsinki, Finland to Warsaw, Poland."

A voice from the radio responds, "This is the control tower. I see your coordinates on air radar."

"I am going to put this down," Harri remarks with worry, looking at Katya.

"No problem. I will call my hairstylist. I will tell her that I can't make my appointment in Warsaw," Katya quips.

The engine noise ceases. All is eerily quiet inside the cockpit. Harri looks intently at the ground and slowly glides the plane.

Katya's expression reveals her fear. The plane slowly glides lower and lower. Then, there are moments of terror as the plane passes close to several buildings and narrowly avoids a large tree.

Harri's expression reveals relief. "It's a miracle. I see a farmer's field ahead. We are going to have a chance to make a safe landing."

The plane descends rapidly. Harri's gaze is focused intently on the ground and the cockpit controls as he attempts to glide the aircraft down to the ground to land. Harri and Katya feel a thud as the wheels bounce on the ground. Both Harri and Katya are violently rocked up and down as the plane's velocity rapidly slows. Everything shakes in the cockpit. It feels as if an earthquake has hit. One wing is clipped by a small tree, which rips the right wing in half and causes the plane to veer to the right as it slows. Then, the plane quickly stops with a jarring thud. All is now quiet in the cockpit for a moment.

Harri looks at Katya in amazement. "Mission accomplished. I planned this all along." He smiles.

"*Joo*. Welcome to Poland! We're still alive," Katya exclaims.

On the Ground in Central Minsk, Belarus

Jaanika sits on the ground, overjoyed with a feeling of victory. She has taken several minutes of footage of the plane circling Minsk. Her car radio is tuned to Minsk Radio. In Russian, the announcer states, "Terrorist elements dropped teddy bears over Minsk skies today. The perpetrators are Americans and their crony allies."

Jaanika is elated. "She uploads the video she has filmed of the teddy bears and the plane onto the Finnish server via Minsk's free Wi-Fi. She starts the car and begins the journey to safety and Poland."

She travels south to the Belarus town of Hrodna and to her ultimate destination of the Kuznica–Brruzgi border crossing to Poland.

Jaanika's automobile progresses closer to Belarus's border control. She observes the line of cars slowing to a crawl.

Jaanika feels apprehensive as she sits in her car waiting for her turn to cross into Poland. As she waits, she sings to herself in Estonian, a language her mother taught her in her youth. Her mother is originally from the small town located outside of Tartu in the south of the country and immigrated to the United States after attending university in Minneapolis.

After twenty minutes, Jaanika's car arrives at the border crossing. A tall man with Slavic features greets her. He is wearing a gray Belarus uniform and carries a gun on his side. "Papers," the guard grunts in badly accented English.

Jaanika presents her passport, which contains her tourist visa. The man scrutinizes her passport along with the visa the Belarus government issued to her in Helsinki.

"Your reason for visiting Belarus?" the guard interrogates.

"Tourism," Jaanika says.

"Where did you go in Belarus?" the guard asks.

"I went to Minsk," Jaanika responds, appearing as innocent as possible.

"Describe for me what places you saw and visited while you were in Minsk," the guard asks.

"Minsk . . . Ah . . . the presidential palace," Jaanika responds hesitantly.

"What did it look like?" the guard asks.

"It was nice and beautiful," Jaanika says.

The guard then returns to his booth and appears to be running Jaanika's name and the license plate of her vehicle in the computer located inside his border patrol station.

Jaanika is overcome with anxiety. She focuses on her mission and calms down.

The border guard returns to the car and gives a nonverbal gesture for her to move her car closer to the border guard station and out of the line to exit Belarus.

She places her foot on the gas pedal, exits the line, and parks the car at the border guard station, which is located several hundred feet away. Jaanika sends a text message to Harri: *I am at the border of Poland and Belarus. I might have some problems leaving the country.*

The border guard walks toward Jaanika's car. He states in Russian, "Please exit the car." He motions with his hand for her to get out of the car.

Fear overcomes Jaanika. She is petrified and can't move. The guard quickly becomes enraged at Jaanika's refusal to leave the car. He swears in Russian. He opens the car door and removes Jaanika from the car by forcefully lifting her arm. He bends her hand to breaking point, picks her up, and drags her to a small detention room located at the back of the guard facility.

Jaanika cries, "I didn't do anything!"

"You here. You stay. Yes. Okay!" the guard yells in English. He then locks the jail door of the small cell.

"You stay here!" the guard yells in accented English.

Jaanika sits alone in a small detention cell located within the guard station. She spends hours inside her small cell. She goes to sleep and is awoken several hours later by another armed man. He escorts her to a nondescript white police van. The door closes behind her. She sits in the back of the windowless van and is transported for several hours.

The bumps of Belarus's dilapidated roads are evident as Jaanika is jostled around as the van travels. Everything is dark inside the van. Jaanika can barely see her hands.

After two hours, the van stops. A guard opens the door and motions for Jaanika to exit. She walks out of the van and is escorted by another Slavic-looking man wearing a gray Belarus uniform, who escorts her to a detention facility.

Upon entering the prison, Jaanika walks through the hallways and is escorted into her cell. She looks around and observes a moldy mattress, a toilet, and one light dangling above the bed. A big black rat momentarily startles Jaanika. It looks her in the eye and slowly walks through the bars of her cell. It seems unfazed by her presence.

Jaanika is alone in a dank, dark, and musty cell in Belarus. Many thoughts race through her mind: *What will happen to me? Will I be tortured, and will I ever see Helsinki and my friends and family?* She then takes a piece of paper out of her pocket, folds it neatly, and puts it in the bottom of her shoe to hide it. She lies on her mattress and stares at the ceiling, hoping to make some sense of a dire situation.

Chapter 2

May 2014

A Spy's Summer Home

The early morning light of the Nordic midsummer sun awakens David from his slumber inside his summerhouse, which is located in a secluded section of the forest outside of Jyväskylä, Finland. David Ivanovich Markoff, a thirty-three-year-old with light blond hair, hazel eyes, and classic Slavic features that betray his Russian background, gets out of bed and appears refreshed from a night of slumber.

"*Huomenta!*" Terhi remarks from the small kitchen two rooms away in the small wooden structure.

"*Houmenta,*" David responds. He gets dressed and walks to the kitchen. Terhi stands next to the window and the sink. She is a petite five-foot-seven, blond-haired, blue-eyed woman. She smiles while preparing the coffee.

"Don't you love Finland's nature?" Terhi inquires and flashes a loving smile.

"My roots may be in rural Russian Karelia, but I was raised in New York City. I guess I am a city man at heart. I have to admit it's beautiful here, though I could do without the giant mosquitoes biting me right now." David puts his arms around Terhi and kisses her.

"You're the one who wanted to move back from the United States. This is our first weekend here, so you better adapt to Finland." Terhi informs him in a demanding tone.

"Hey, why not come with me for a jog in the woods?" David suggests. David walks to the kitchen drawer, opens it, and takes out a 357 Magnum handgun.

"What is that for?" Terhi looks at him, a little puzzled.

"It is for emergencies. It's just in case we run into an angry bear of the Russian kind or an angry moose of the Finnish kind, for that matter," David retorts and smiles slyly.

"You see threats everywhere," Terhi quips, looking a little annoyed.

Terhi and David are startled by the sounds of glass breaking in the cabin. Numerous projectiles begin penetrating the cabin walls and windows. Terhi drops to the floor. David dives to the ground to take cover. He crawls to Terhi's body as glass continues to break from piercing bullets raining down on his head. He examines Terhi and spots a small bullet hole near her forehead. Terhi is unconscious, and her body seems lifeless and cold. The sounds of bullets flying in the air continue unabated around the cabin.

David's heart is racing, and adrenaline continues to rush through his veins like an endless river. He crawls as close to the floor as he can. He plants his right elbow and moves his body forward. Then, he plants his left elbow and drags his feet along as fast as he can. He is carrying his handgun safely in his back pocket, and he slowly heads for the back door of the cabin. The sound of gunfire and the smell of gunpowder permeate the air. He hears the voices of men talking in a foreign language that he can't identify. He soon arrives at his destination. Fear fills his body.

With terror permeating his being, he decides to flee the cabin and make a break for his car. With his gun firmly gripped within his right hand, he flings the door open with his left hand and springs up in a desperate race to save his life and to reach his parked car, which is located only fifteen yards from the house.

He runs and rapidly fires the gun in the direction of the cabin with his left hand, where the snipers appear to be firing at him. The pops of numerous shots from the barrel of David's weapon echo in the distance. David's arms pump rapidly, sweat drips down his forehead, and he feels breathless as he exhales and inhales rapidly. He reaches the car and quickly opens the car door. He jumps inside and closes the door. From inside the car, bullets can be heard hitting the car in rapid succession, making a ringing sound within the car as they penetrate the aluminum body.

David's hands are shaking as he nervously puts the key inside the ignition and turns it. The engine starts. He quickly presses on the accelerator and drives away from the cabin as rapidly as he can. The car swiftly accelerates from forty to eighty miles an hour. He drives down a dirt road, which turns up a trail of dust and rocks in his wake. The sound of sporadic gunfire continues well down the road. David thinks he has lost the gunmen tailing him, but he continues to drive on the dirt road at a fast pace.

David turns onto the highway and stops at a small gasoline station. With his shaking hand, he takes his spare cell phone out of the glove compartment of the car and makes a call.

Several rings can be heard. "United States Embassy. Jake McMillian speaking."

"This is David. Call an ambulance for me. Terhi has been shot, and my cabin is riddled with bullet holes!" David yells with worry.

"Are you okay? What happened?" Jake questions.

"Someone is out to eliminate me. I am unhurt. Get someone out to my cabin quickly! I don't think Terhi has much time," David announces.

"I will call the police. Let me know your location. Did you see anything?" Jake questions.

"No, I just ran out of the cabin and fired in the opposite direction. I am not sure who did it. It could have been Russian SVR or the Chinese, as they are the only agencies with the capability to launch an operation in Finland."

"I will get help. I will call Langley, too. Sit tight for a moment. As a CIA employee, you should know the drill," Jake informs him.

"Terhi is not in good condition," David says. His voice reeks of an inner agony.

David sits in his car. He is somber and silent as he contemplates what happened. Thoughts race through his mind: *Was it my position that put Terhi in danger? Should I have run? Who could have caused this?*

Chapter 3

CIA's Helsinki Station

The alarm of David's clock rings at 6:00 a.m. A month has elapsed since the shooting incident at his summer cabin. The nightly replay of Terhi's death within David's dreams has subsided, though the feeling of guilt for letting it happen has not. The "white nights" are evident in Helsinki as David rises out of bed and is shocked out of his semi-awake, groggy state into consciousness by the bright light of the sun shining into his apartment at such an early hour.

David gets out of bed and showers. He dresses in his diplomatic business attire and walks out of his new apartment located in the Kallio section of Helsinki. He heads to another day of work at the United States embassy. He walks in the direction of central Kallio's Bear Park. Once in the park, David waits for his tram to arrive and transport him south to Helsinki's city center, which is near the United States embassy.

The tram arrives, and David boards it. He walks to the middle of the vehicle and takes a seat. He hopes that his position on the tram will provide a good view of all individuals who board and exit and ensure no one is watching or following him undetected. David is especially wary since no one has been caught in connection with the attack at his summer home. He is diligent to evade detection by using the good intelligence tradecraft he learned at the CIA. David knows to avoid using all compromised technology, which includes unsecured phone calls, the Internet, and all social media. When using a false name, passport, or identity, he plays the part at all times. This means no phone calls home, few friends outside of the CIA, and only answering to his false name.

David conducts a visual survey of the tram to spot signs of surveillance. He looks in back of the tram and sees nothing out of the ordinary. He sees a businessman wearing a suit and tie who is reading email on his smartphone, a young woman sitting with a small child, and a university student possessing dark hair who is reading her smartphone and listening to music. He looks in front of the tram and sees no sign that anyone has followed him on to the train. He checks outside the tram and notices no one is watching or could be recording him. He then looks under his seat and sees no sign of unusual electronic devices. David concludes that all seems normal, though his paranoia continues unabated. David knows that surveillance can be in electronic form, which is harder to detect. David is aware that an intelligence officer's life can be a precarious existence filled with paranoia and constant doubt. He has become innately skeptical of everyone's motivations and all information provided to him as a result of his intelligence work.

The tram moves forward and progresses in the direction of central Helsinki. David takes out his Department of State-issued cell phone from his briefcase. He turns on the device and quickly opens an email sent from his Department of State supervisor, Edith, which is marked urgent. He reads it: *You are now scheduled for an interview with a man who has a United States citizen-related issue. See me when you arrive at work, as this is a high-interest case.*

The tram approaches Stockmann's, a well-known department store in Helsinki. David reaches for the button and presses it, which signals to the driver that he wants to leave the tram at the next stop. The tram proceeds to stop. David exits and walks a mile in the direction of the Baltic Sea and the United States embassy. As a rule, David always changes his route to avoid detection from surveillance conducted by the Finnish Security Intelligence Service, Russian intelligence, or anyone who might want to do him harm. The sail-like edifice of the embassy complex comes into view. David reaches the building's entrance, shows his identification to the guard, walks into the embassy, and heads in the direction of his office.

On his way, David spots his CIA supervisor, Jake, who is six feet two inches tall, possesses blond hair and blue eyes, and appears slightly overweight. He is wearing a blue suit and tie and is accompanied by another bald, athletic-looking man. "Good morning,

Jake. How is it going?" David remarks. David shakes hands with Jake.

"Very good. Again, I want to offer my condolences on the death of your wife," Jake says.

"Thank you for your thoughts," David states.

"Are you enjoying the white nights of Finland? It can be very hard to sleep during this time of year when the sun does not set until 1:00 a.m.," Jake questions.

"I can't complain," David says.

"I want you to meet Ambassador Cliff Armstrong. This is David Markoff. He just arrived recently from Washington DC." The ambassador puts out his hand to shake. He is six feet tall, bald, with brown eyes, a thick, muscular neck, and a huge bodybuilder-like appearance.

"Good to meet you, Mr. Ambassador. I hear many compliments about your athletic abilities," Dave remarks. David is aware that the ambassador is a former professional boxer and that his primary credentials for his job were bundling checks for the president's campaign.

"I think my abilities are very overrated, but thank you," the United States ambassador reaches his hand out to shake. David shakes the ambassador's hand firmly.

"I hear your family is from Russia originally. Is that true?" the ambassador inquires.

"Yes, that is correct. My family is from a small town located near the Finnish–Russian border called Vyborg. It is located in the Russian province of Karelia," David remarks. He smiles politely.

"We need to talk at some point. Russian culture is of great interest to me," Ambassador Armstrong says. He flashes a big grin.

"We have to attend a meeting, but I hope to see you around the embassy," Jake remarks. Jake and the US ambassador proceed to walk down the stairs toward the ambassador's office.

David walks into the Consular Office and meets Edith in her office. The office possesses several windows that provide a strategic view of the Baltic Sea. There are pictures of her family placed on her desk, along with scenic areas of Washington DC. Placed on the walls, Edith has several pictures of Manila, which was her last Department of State assignment.

"Good morning, Edith," David remarks with a smile.

"Hope your morning was good, too," Edith states.

"Not bad. I just saw Ambassador Armstrong walk by our coffee shop this morning. He seems to be a nice guy."

Edith motions for David to sit down. "He is a very pleasant person to work with. Listen, Jake has recommended that you should be in charge of interviewing a Finnish man who is the Outlandish PR CEO. Have you heard of him?" Edith questions.

"No." David appears a little puzzled.

"He is Harri Bergstrom, a well-known activist for human rights and left-wing causes. He has been very critical of the United States in the past. It seems he is reporting an issue related to an American citizen living in Helsinki who is now located in Belarus and is associated with the teddy bear bombing incident. I want you to obtain all the information you can about Harri and the woman. We don't have a United States embassy operating in Belarus, so we are in charge of this political hot potato."

"Thanks for your confidence in me. Did anyone get hurt in the teddy bear bombing of Minsk?" David asks.

"Just Belarus's dictator President Lukashenka's ego. Several of his intelligence officials and military were demoted for letting a small aircraft fly over Minsk unimpeded. I hear it has encouraged the opposition, as the government is looking like a laughing stock now. This really angered the Russians. It made Belarus look as though it was unable to control its borders. You may not be aware that Russia has a close alliance with Belarus and views the country as part of its military security plan," Edith informs him.

"I will do my best," David retorts. He gets up from his seat and walks out of Edith's office. David then walks down to the embassy's Foggy Bottom Café, which is named for Department of State's Washington DC headquarters' nickname, "Foggy Bottom." He purchases a medium coffee and curses himself for his coffee addiction, which he only picked up from working long hours at CIA headquarters and visiting the coffee shop too often.

Dave brings his coffee to his desk. He logs on to his computer and checks his email. The phone rings. He picks up the phone.

"Hello," David answers.

"Hey, this is Jake. Bergstrom is going to meet you in the conference room. Get back to me after you interview him. Thanks."

"No problem," David responds.

David walks to the main conference room, sits down, sets up his laptop to type notes, and waits for Bergstrom to be escorted up to his floor.

The room possesses pictures of Washington DC, an American flag standing in the corner, and a window with a view of the Baltic Sea and Helsinki Harbor. The wooden desk is stark and minimalist in design.

Harri Bergstrom saunters into the room. He is wearing a polo shirt and jeans, has a small goatee, possesses a laptop computer, and carries a smartphone strapped to his waist. His manner denotes a hip, Nordic startup.

David stands up and puts out his hand to shake. "Welcome to the United States embassy, Helsinki. I hear you are here to report a problem associated with a United States citizen."

Harri smiles. "I have never met a United States bureaucrat before."

"We are human also. Why not sit down and we can talk." David smiles and gives a nonverbal gesture for Harri to sit. He pauses. "I hope you don't mind, but I will be typing the notes of our meeting as we talk. I want to make sure I get all the details correct."

Harri sits down. "Let me see those notes in the end. I am suspicious of the United States government. You know, all those NSA revelations."

David queries, "I can let you look at them if you would like. What brings you to the embassy today?"

"Well, I am here to discuss Jaanika Olson. She is a United States citizen who was living in Finland and attending the University of Helsinki. I think she is also a citizen of Estonia," Harri says.

"Was she registered with the embassy? Many Americans who live outside the United States register with the local United States embassy so that their family members may be alerted if there is an emergency or they need assistance from the United States government," David informs.

"I'm not sure, but I doubt she would," Harri asserts. "I think she probably demonstrated against United States policies and tries to stay away from the United States government if she can help it," Harri adds.

"It seems that Jaanika has been arrested in Belarus and is now in the custody of its notorious security service, the KGB. I'm hoping that you can assist us in obtaining her release from prison," Harri says as David types his notes on his laptop.

"Can you provide the details of what happened to her?" David inquires.

"Sure. She was at the border of Poland and Belarus and disappeared," Harri remarks.

"When was your last communication with her?" David asks. He intently types Harri's response on his laptop.

"It was on July fourth. I received a text from her indicating that she was having problems crossing the border from Belarus into Poland," Harri says.

"Do you know what was she doing in Belarus?" David questions. He continues to type furiously on his laptop.

"Jaanika was assisting us in our efforts to publicize the country's lack of respect for human rights," Harri remarked, looking serious.

"Have you informed her relatives?" David asks. He looks up from his laptop.

"Not yet. I am attempting to obtain the names now," Harri adds.

"Can you describe what she was doing exactly?" David asks. He returns to looking at his laptop and typing.

"She was helping with the logistics, which were related to our flight," Harri adds.

"Was she doing anything else?" David asks.

"No," Harri retorts. His expression indicates he is a little upset.

"Who else was involved with your efforts to illegally enter Belarus airspace and drop teddy bears from a plane?" David questions.

"I don't think this is any of the United States government's business." Harri's expression reveals he is annoyed.

"Listen. I am just trying to assist in obtaining information to help a United States citizen. I'm not the CIA . . . or the FBI, for that matter." David looks up from his laptop and flashes a sincere smile.

"You're all CIA as far as I am concerned. Do you have a way to contact your office in Belarus?" Harri asks. He sits back in his chair with his arms folded and an angry expression.

"We only have an interest section open at the Swiss embassy in Belarus currently. As you probably know, Lukashenko has broken relations with the United States. We will do all we can," David says.

"Can you tell me anything else about the incident?" David questions.

"She was stopped at the border. I know the Belarus authorities, which control the country, are not happy about us embarrassing them by dropping teddy bears and flyers stating 'Freedom.' I'm not sure if they know she was involved," Harri says.

"Listen, I'm pretty ignorant about what happened. What did you do in Belarus exactly?" David asks. He knows playing dumb never hurts when attempting to gain the most information possible from a source.

"We flew a plane and dropped teddy bears and flyers over central Minsk," Harri says.

"Was this funded by your company?" David asks. He flashes an inquisitive expression.

"I am not going into detail. This is a sensitive subject in Finland and internationally. I will provide you with Jaanika's address in Finland and that of her relatives in the United States. I'm fed up with your inquiry at this point. I need help for Jaanika!" Harri says.

"Here is my card. Please forward the information to my address. At the Department of State, we are here to help you." David takes his card out and hands it to Harri.

Both Harri and David walk out of the room, and David escorts him to the United States embassy's exit. Harri walks outside the embassy and gets into a black BMW.

United States Embassy, Helsinki, Finland

David then walks to the security officer's office. He puts his card in the card-reader slot. After a few seconds' delay, the door opens. He makes sure no one in the Consular Office has seen him, as he does not want his CIA cover to be blown by United States diplomats, who are known to speak too much after consuming a few glasses of wine.

He sees Jake, the undercover CIA chief of station and David's boss. "Hey, busy time with the ambassador?" David quips.

"Just giving the daily brief. It's one of my many duties here at the embassy," Jake reports.

"Have you heard anything from the Finnish police about the murder investigation?" Jake inquires.

"Nothing yet, unfortunately. I passed a polygraph to prove it was not me," David says.

"Anything from CIA headquarters about how long this assignment will last?" David inquires.

"No, you have been detailed indefinitely at our Helsinki station. This is your permanent home now, so I hope you like the dark Nordic winters and the rainy, cold, and depressing weather. What exactly happened at CIA headquarters? It's pretty odd having an analyst on duty in Helsinki. We are a small, unimportant regional CIA office in Helsinki," Jake questions.

"I received operational training and was ready to become an operations officer who engages in real spy work, like recruiting sources and designing operations, but ended up being assigned to the Counter Terrorism Center as a South Asia analyst at CIA headquarters writing reports. You know the United States government can be illogical at times. All I can say is that my Russian background is not popular at the CIA now. I guess I have been exiled," David says. He flashes an unhappy expression.

"How did you get into the CIA by the way? You don't seem like the typical employee here. Who recruited you?" Jake asks.

"Actually, I found the cia.gov site and sent my application in. I was interviewed and, a year later, entered on as an employee. I guess I wanted adventure and to prove I was a real American. I discovered this was more of a job for bureaucratic types, and my past seems to be more important than my ability to do the job," David says. His expression reveals he is quite frustrated.

"Interesting. Let's not dwell on your assignment or on your past. Let's get back to our person of interest, Harri Berg. What other details were you able to extract?" Jake asks.

"Well, Harri carried out the operation with two other people. The American involved was caught at the border. There were no indications that other organizations or groups were involved, from his statements he gave to me today," David says.

"Did you know that the Belarus authorities have issued an international Interpol arrest warrant for all those involved in this plane flight?" Jake informs.

"Actually, I was not aware of this. This is the first I heard about the event. Will Finland extradite those involved with the Belarus teddy bear incident to Belarus?" David questions.

"It does not appear it will happen. Belarus and Finland do not have good diplomatic relations due to Alexander Lukashenko's poor human rights record. This is likely causing Russia to become really angry, as Belarus is their satellite now. They are blaming Finland for this proactive act," Jake adds.

"What else is being reported on the high side? You know . . . at the top-secret level?" David questions.

"Nothing really. I know that Belarus is pretty upset about the incident, and several high-ranking individuals in Lukashenko's upper ranks have been demoted. I get the feeling that the Finnish government knew something about it beforehand. Harri is connected to the high-ranking members of the Social Democratic Party and Finland's prime minister, who is a Center Party member," Jake says.

"That is an interesting link," David adds.

"Do you know any details about who funded the operation?" Jake questions.

"I attempted to obtain all the details with several questions I posed to him, but he shut me down," David briefs.

"Thanks. I know you have to brief Consular Affairs about your interview. Please say nothing about our meeting, of course, as we don't want to compromise your cover in Finland working as a CIA officer. No one in the Department of State should know," Jake warns.

"No problem. I know all the operational procedures for covered positions," David says.

David walks out of the security office and heads to see Edith in Consular Affairs. He arrives at Edith's office door and knocks.

"May I enter?" David asks.

"Sure. Come in and sit down," Edith responds. She smiles politely and points to the seat in front of her desk.

David takes a seat in front of Edith's desk.

"Edith, I just wanted to inform you that I met with Harri. I will provide you with all the details of my interview. He is going to send me an email with Jaanika Olson's relatives' names."

"Thanks for getting on top of the issue." Edith smiles approvingly.

"So much for a slow diplomatic post in the Nordic countries," David quips. He then rises from his chair, walks out of Edith's office, returns to his cube, and logs back onto his computer.

David checks his email and discovers that George at CIA headquarters has sent another email. David opens the email using encryption software: *The CIA has uncovered several Russian spies working in its headquarters in Langley. They may think you are connected to them.* Worry and paranoia grips David suddenly, despite his having done nothing. He feels a little nervous.

David quickly opens another email that was sent from Jake. The email states, *Here is a picture of Jaanika.* David downloads the attachment and views Jaanika Olson's profile. David is shocked and his eyes open wide, which reveals his disbelief. He recognizes the picture. She is his cousin, whom he saw in Minneapolis over a decade ago at a wedding.

Helsinki, Finland

Harri is sitting in his BMW, driving north from the Koviposti section of Helsinki. The radio in his car is blaring techno music as Harri drives at an excessive speed to his next destination.

Harri makes a call while driving. He presses a button on his phone, and several rings can be heard on the speaker. A person picks up. "Hey, Katya. I just talked with the consular officer at the United States embassy. I am not sure if they are going to be able to assist us much. By the way, is all the money ready?"

Harri's car stops at the traffic light. In a moment, the car is rocked by a huge explosion and consumed with heat and fire. The windows of the car blow out. The hood of the car blows off its hinges as a huge fireball envelops the car. Harri quickly loses consciousness as life slips from his body.

"Harri! Are you okay?" Katya cries in Finnish as she hears the explosion on the other end of the phone.

Chapter 4

The Prime Minister's Meeting

Helsinki, Finland

Inside a building in central Helsinki, which contains elements of classic Swedish imperial design, lies Finland's prime minister's office. A windowless room, which possesses a map of the world and clocks indicating the time in Brussels, Berlin, London, Moscow, and Washington DC, is the situation headquarters for the Finnish prime minister. Within the room, tables possessing the attributes of classic wooden Scandinavian design are placed strategically, video monitors are mounted on the walls, and Alvar Alto-designed chairs give the room a modernist appearance. In walks Prime Minister Tarja Manninen. She is thirty-five years old, and her auburn hair is stylishly cut. She is wearing rimless glasses and has on a blue business suit. She sits down at the head of the table, emitting an aura of authority. Two men are sitting on either side of the table. Both are in their forties. They stand up as a sign of respect and then sit down. One man, Timo Holgrum, heads the Finnish Defense Forces. He is bald; wears a military uniform, which consists of a blue suit, tie, a red collar insignia and has numerous military decorations hanging from his left lapel. Across the table from him sits Jarmo

Bergstrom, the Finnish Security Intelligence Service director. He has blond hair and is wearing a gray–blue suit, purple rimless glasses, and a blue spotted tie with a small pin that contains a lion standing atop a sword.

"Good afternoon. The Russians have sent a diplomatic letter to my office threatening revenge in response to the teddy bear flight in Belarus. They view this as a Finnish invasion of their Belarus satellite. They want a response from us within two weeks," Tarja says. "What is the state of readiness of the Finnish defense forces?" she questions and looks at Timo.

"In response to your orders to increase our defense posture, we have added more troops at the eastern border. The Russians are increasing their air force sorties from their base in Karelia. In Helsinki, our air force is on standby, and we have patrols in the Baltic Sea on heightened alert," Timo reports.

Tarja looks at Jarmo. "What do you think the Russians may do?" She appears quite concerned.

"Russian President Vladimirovich is clearly bent on revenge. He is intent on another military operation after Ukraine. Finland or Estonia could be the next target. This may be an excuse for an invasion of Finland. Clearly, the Russian president wants Finland back in its control. The teddy bear flight may be the excuse for Russian troops to cross the border or take over the Aland Islands in the Baltic," Jarmo warns.

"I may seek the help of NATO and Sweden. Keep me updated. I will brief President Koivu," Tarja says. She stands up and walks out of the room.

Chapter 5

Day 10 in Amerikanka Prison

Jaanika sits motionless in her small cell, which reeks of urine and mold. The summer heat has made the conditions seem unbearable. A small bucket to be used as a toilet, which is located in a corner of the cell, is indescribably putrid and emits an awful stench. A small basin is located in the corner, there is a narrow window of matted glass, and a prominent document is posted in Russian on the wall; Jaanika guesses it may be the prison's rules. The cell is shaped like a coffin. It appears that Jaanika has not eaten for several days. Her whole body seems to ache from the lack of oxygen inside the prison. Under her eyes are dark lines, which reveal her sleep deprivation. There is sweat pouring down her face and perspiration dampening her clothes.

The silence and isolation of her cell are broken by the sounds of the footsteps of an unknown individual approaching. The sounds echo louder and louder within her cell.

Jaanika peers nervously outside the bars of her cell. A man in a gray uniform who has classic Slavic features walks toward the cell and is clearly discernible despite the corridor being dimly lit. He possesses light blond hair, hazel eyes, and a pronounced chin. He is five-eleven and wears a lapel pin that has a silver sword; a red, green, and blue crest; and the Russian letters KGB clearly marked.

"I am Ivan Mikhailovich. Jaanika, can you please walk with me?" He flashes a stern smile and unlocks and opens the cell door. His words and his distinct English accent reveal his United Kingdom university education.

Jaanika possesses an anxious smile and rises slowly from the ground. She proceeds to walk out of her cell and limps slowly as she progresses barefoot down a small, white corridor that is dimly lit. After about five minutes, they both arrive at a small door. The KGB officer opens it, revealing a small white room with a number of tables. Both Jaanika and Ivan enter the room. Jaanika looks a little worried, but she staggers into the chair. A masked male guard quietly enters the room and sits next to Ivan.

"Please sit down. Welcome to Amerikanka prison. This prison is named for America, where you were born," Ivan states. He reaches to his briefcase and takes out a can of soda. He places the soda in front of Jaanika and says nothing.

Jaanika thinks to herself about how to play this situation. *Should I act dumb or provide some information?* She tries to assess what the KGB knows.

Jaanika fidgets with her hair for a moment to defuse the tension.

"Now tell me. What is your name?" Ivan questions.

"Jaanika Olson. I would like to talk to the United States embassy," she retorts and seems a bit disoriented, but she grabs the drink placed next to her and takes a sip.

"What was your reason for entering Belarus?" Ivan questions in a friendly manner.

"Tourism. I would like to talk to my family," Jaanika adds. She sits up in her chair and seems to have regained her composure. Color returns to her cheeks. She thinks of her grandfather's courage during his KGB arrest under Soviet dictator Joseph Stalin and is reenergized. She remembers her grandfather stating that, "Nothing happens by chance in a KGB prison."

"Jaanika, I have to be honest with you. We have analyzed your telephonic and Internet communications in Belarus. We know you uploaded the video of the plane and the teddy bears dropping over Minsk onto your computer server in Finland," Ivan retorts.

Jaanika is shocked and silent for a moment. She regains her composure. "I just saw the plane. I thought it was unusual. I uploaded it." Jaanika flashes an angry expression.

"Now, what was your real reason for visiting Belarus?" Ivan questions in an ominous manner.

"Tourism," Jaanika responds forcefully. She crosses her arms.

"We have to know the truth. Were you involved with the individuals who dropped those teddy bears and flyers from a plane?" Ivan asks. He seems quite angry.

"I want to talk to my family," Jaanika demands. She avoids eye contact with Ivan.

"Fine. I want you to think about what your real reason for visiting Belarus actually was. You will sit in the cell until you tell us the truth. Those who do not cooperate do not receive any privileges in Amerikanka," Ivan warns.

"What am I charged with?" Jaanika asks.

"You are being held for questioning by the Belarus government," Ivan retorts. "Listen, I can be your friend. I understand your reasoning for participating with the flight. You want to help the people of Belarus. Let me know why you did it, and I will understand. All will be forgiven." Ivan smiles slyly.

"I want to talk to a lawyer. I'm an American citizen," Jaanika demands. She leans back in her chair with a body posture that reveals her defiance.

There is silence in the room for a minute as Jaanika says nothing, and Ivan looks at her with an expression revealing that he is quite perturbed. Tension fills the air.

Ivan looks at the guard for minute. "Very well, Jaanika. If things do not go well for you, then it's your actions that made your Belarus experience unpleasant. Most cells here have ten people residing in them and contain no mattresses. We will transfer you to a less comfortable cell if you do not cooperate," Ivan mentions with a stern look. He then motions for a guard to remove Jaanika.

The masked guard proceeds to handcuff Jaanika. He then bends her arms back so that she can see only the concrete floor. The guard walks her out of the room and walks back to the cell. Jaanika screams in great pain on the way to her cell. "I want to talk to a lawyer!"

Ivan walks out of the detention center and heads to his parked car. He then enters his vehicle. In his car, Ivan hears the tone of his cell phone signaling an incoming call. Ivan takes the phone out of his pocket and answers it. "Ivan, you have to report to headquarters in Minsk. I need to talk to you."

"Yes, sir. I will report as soon as I can," Ivan responds in deference to a high official.

Ivan travels in his car down the winding roads outside of Minsk to the center of town. As he enters central Minsk, the city seems spotlessly clean and contains statues of Lenin and Marx and drab grayish buildings built in the 1950s and 1960s. On Karl Marx Street, which is the central avenue of the city near where the KGB headquarters is located, are international American-owned fast food and coffee shops and fancy boutiques. This contrasts with the rest of the country, which is clearly stuck in Soviet times with its shoddy, undeveloped roads, lack of electricity, and dilapidated infrastructure.

Ivan parks his car. He then enters the imposing yellow KGB headquarters, which is designed with imposing Greek columns and is surrounded by a vacant plaza and statues celebrating former Soviet-era KGB and NKVD leaders. He walks through a labyrinth of drab, white halls lit with florescent lights. People wearing KGB uniforms pass him by. Ivan salutes superior officers as they pass while he heads toward his destination.

Ivan enters an elevator and takes it up to the fifth floor of the building. He seems apprehensive. He opens the door marked "General Secretary" and sees a woman sitting up front at the desk.

Ivan walks up to the front desk. "I'm Ivan Mikhailovich, and am here to see Valerie."

The secretary picks up the phone and calls her supervisor. After a minute, she responds in Russian, "You can go in."

Ivan opens the door to reveal a large room that contains pictures of various high-ranking KGB officers on the walls. Valerie stands up, smiles, and motions for Ivan to sit down.

"Greetings, Ivan. Sit down," Valerie states.

"Yes, sir," Ivan responds. He sits at the chair adjacent to Valerie's desk.

"So, how is the questioning of the American going so far?" he asks, expecting a detailed report.

"Sir, we have questioned her but have no clear indication if she was a part of the teddy bear bombing incident," Ivan responds.

"I know you attended school in the United Kingdom, so I think I have to tell you to not go about this in the traditional manner. We need a confession. You are going to have to up the pressure on Jaanika. Lukashenko is extremely unhappy about this. His master in Moscow, President Vladimirovich, is furious at the Finns," Valerie says, looking quite serious.

"No problem," Ivan responds.

"We also need you to assist us with an operation in Finland. It's highly secret and involves your specific skill set," Valerie says.

Both are quiet for a moment. Valerie is intently viewing a file lying in front of him.

"The boss is looking for heads to roll. Frankly, I think another purge inside the Belarus government is in play here. Your successful operation will ensure that your head does not roll for the teddy bears." Valerie pauses for a second. "You know, Ivan, those Finns think they are safe from Russian retribution in Helsinki. They will have to pay a price for anti-Belarus provocations. We have to show that they will not be safe, even though the Soviets did not succeed in 1939 or 1943. The Russian President Vladimirovich does not shoot his best generals like Stalin did back then," Valerie states. He pounds his fist on his table, revealing his anger.

"I am more than happy to organize an operation. I think you will be pleased," Ivan says. He smiles confidently.

"Make the boss happy, and I will be happy also. I will send the operation details and the funds," Valerie says.

"Valerie, you know we have been friends for decades. Can I speak freely?" Ivan asks, sitting in his chair.

"Yes, Ivan." Valerie sits at his desk. He puts down his pen and file and listens quietly.

"You are a national hero. The economic situation is really bad in the country, and the president is no longer popular. Perhaps this incident may open up an opportunity for a change, with you taking a lead," Ivan mentions. He sits back in his chair, nervously awaiting an answer.

Valerie sits quietly and looks at Ivan for a second. "I hear what you are saying. I have thought about this. I will get in touch with you if things develop. Succeed in your mission. It's important for both of us."

"Sir, thank you." Ivan gets up from his chair and salutes.

Valerie smiles and points him in the direction of the door.

He walks out of the room, down the hall, and returns to his office within the KGB headquarters. His mind is filled with the beginning of a plan to save his career and his life.

Chapter 6

A Meeting with a Source

"The truth is never simple and always changes," David quips while sitting in his secure office talking to Jake in the United States embassy in Helsinki.

"That is why they pay you the big bucks," Jake says. He chuckles a little. "Well, maybe the relatively moderate amount of dollars." Jake flashes a friendly grin again. "Listen, David, I need to know if this man is going to provide reliable information," Jake adds.

"What is the background and biography of this potential source?" David inquires. David takes a pad of paper from his desk drawer and starts writing.

"He is a failed asylum seeker in Finland. The Finnish immigration system has a backlog of people to deport now that the country is being deluged with refugees originating from the Middle East and Afghanistan. Our source is caught in lengthy legal appeals after being denied asylum in Finland at the lower legal level. Our source wants status in the United States and is also asking for money for his information. That seems to be the primary motivation for providing information to the United States government. You may uncover other reasons when you interview him," Jake informs.

"So, I need to talk to him. What's our goal in this case? He sounds like he is an unvetted source. These are a dime a dozen in the intelligence world and not taken very seriously. I'd rather recruit some sources with better access to information," David says. He looks a little disappointed.

Jake sports a friendly smile. "David, that is nonsense. He could provide you with great intelligence. You have to earn your money in this case. Talk to him and get your sense if he may be a good source. Don't let the fact that he is unvetted, having walked into the embassy to provide information, become prejudicial to your judgment. I don't need to tell you that HUMIT, running human sources, is a delicate business. You have to be patient to snag a good source in Helsinki. However, there is lots of potential in Finland. You have all the operatives represented here: Russian Foreign Intelligence (SVR), the Iranian MOIS, the Iranian-backed Hezbollah, Ethiopian Intelligence, the Israeli MOSSAD, and India's RAW. It's all about recruiting the right people: those who possess access to valuable information and have defined, knowable motivations. You know that it's all a game, and Finland is your playground now," Jake adds. He sits down at his desk and starts to sip his cup of coffee.

"I get it. So, where will I meet this potential source?" David inquires. He continues writing studiously on his notepad, though he feels like Jake is putting a pretty face on a bad situation.

"David, you need to head to a coffee shop near the center of Helsinki. It's called Esplandi Café. Marshal Carl Gustaf Mannerheim, who is one of the key figures in Finnish history, would hang out there. It's nice. Our source thinks he is talking to a United States government official. He does not know you work for the CIA. Also, remember, bring back a receipt, as CIA headquarters will hand me my ass on a platter for not documenting expenses," Jake says.

"Got it," David says. He smiles confidently. David knows that recruiting good sources is the key to a successful CIA career. An unvetted source, derided as a walk-in, is a hard sell, and CIA headquarters will not view his information seriously.

Two hours later, David walks out of the embassy and into a café. He searches for the source. The café is a landmark in the center of Helsinki. It contains beautiful paintings and has an imperial Swedish design and large, ornate tables.

David spots a dark-skinned, Middle Eastern-looking man who is sitting at a corner table. He looks quite nervous and apprehensive.

David approaches the man at the table. "Are you Ibrahim?" David inquires.

"Yes. I'm Ibrahim. You're the American, no?"

"Yes. Let's talk. You informed a guard at the United States embassy of information about a threat," David inquires. He pulls out a chair from the table, sits down, and takes out a notepad from his briefcase.

"Yes, I have information about a possible terrorist." He looks quite nervous. "I want legal status in the United States, though," he says and begins to peer around the room in fear of something or someone unknown.

"Let's review all that you know. I'm not sure I am aware of all the information you provided to the guard at the embassy," David remarks. He looks quite serious. "So, where are you from originally?" David asks.

"Tehran, Iran," Ibrahim says. He coughs a little and takes out a handkerchief from his pocket to cover his mouth.

"What was your profession while living in Iran?" David asks.

"I worked in a government office in the Ministry of Trade in the government of Iran. My job was to promote our agricultural products in Lebanon, Syria, and the Gulf States," Ibrahim says.

"Why did you travel to Finland? This place does not seem a popular destination for Iranians to live," David asks. He is writing furiously on his notepad. David closely observes Ibrahim's eyes and other body gestures to determine whether he is telling the truth and to assess whether he might be hiding information from him.

"I found Christ. I converted to Christianity and experienced lots of problems in Tehran due to my faith. The Iranian police arrested and tortured me. They demanded that I renounce my religion. I possessed a valid visa for Finland at the time, as I had been in Helsinki for an international conference a year ago. I managed to escape prison, cross the Iranian border, and took a plane flight here," Ibrahim says.

"What information do you want to provide to the United States government?" David asks. He looks up from his notepad.

"I have made a friend in Helsinki. He lives near me and approached me several times to assist him. I think he must work with the Iranian intelligence service or as a Hezbollah agent. He stated that he hates Americans and Israelis and wants to strike them in Finland. He seems very secretive," Ibrahim says. He scans the café worriedly.

"Tell me, when will this attack occur?" David inquires.

"I'm not sure. A couple of weeks ago, I talked to the man," Ibrahim says.

"Can you provide his name and the date of your discussion? Do you remember any other details?" David asks.

"I met him several months ago. I was living in refugee housing in Helsinki. He operates an illegal cab service and sells fake goods on the street here. I was in need of a job, and he started to engage in a conversation with me, as he knew I was interested. We later went out together, and he shared this information to see if I could assist him. His name is Isfahan," Ibrahim briefs.

"Did he tell you what the targets were or provide any date for when he intended to carry out the operation?" David asks.

"I remember he was talking about the Jewish synagogue here in Helsinki, an Israeli shop, and an American business," Ibrahim added.

"Do you meet him regularly?" David asks. He continues to furiously write down the details.

"He sends texts to me, and then we meet. We got together at a falafel place, which is located near the University of Helsinki's city center campus," Ibrahim says.

"What is this man's address?" David inquires.

"I remember some of it but have to obtain the full address later. I don't speak much Finnish. My English is not too good either," Ibrahim says.

"What do you want in return for the information you are providing to the United States government?" David asks.

"I want legal status in the United States. They will deport me back to Iran. I can't go back there. I am also in need of cash. I can't work legally in Finland, and the funds Finland provides to asylum seekers are not much," Ibrahim says. He looks quite distressed.

"You realize if you are lying to me that this will have ramifications for you," David warns.

"Yes. I am telling you the truth. This is what I know," Ibrahim states. He smiles worriedly and seems to be sweating and nervous.

"Did you report this information to the Finnish Police or the Finnish Security Intelligence Service?" David asks.

"No. I am having so many problems with Finnish immigration. I don't want to talk to them," Ibrahim says.

"We will be in touch soon." David stands up and shakes hands with the man. He gets up from the table and walks out of the café. David walks down the street. A man appears from the side of the café and begins to follow David. The person is wearing a leather jacket, possesses a full beard, and appears to be over six feet tall.

David looks back nervously and spots a man walking behind him. David begins to walk faster as he crosses through several intersections in central Helsinki. He abruptly turns left at the intersection. He looks back and, worrying, sees the same man getting closer and appearing to approach him.

David begins to run down the street in a full sprint. He dodges several cars and runs through an alleyway between two apartment blocks. He peers behind him and sees that the man is continuing to follow him, trailing by only a few hundred meters.

David arrives at another intersection. He spots a cab and immediately hails it. The car stops. David enters the car.

"Please take me to the United States embassy quickly," David orders.

"*Joo!*" the Finnish driver says. The car begins to accelerate quickly.

David sees the man who was following him standing on the corner. He attempts to take a picture of the man with his phone's camera, but his phone refuses to work. David is frustrated by this development. He looks out the window and momentarily sees the man's eyes staring at him ominously with clearly ill intentions. David wonders if the man is connected to the attempt on his life at the summer home or is an Iranian-connected Hezbollah operative. Perspiration is running down David's face. He calls Jake.

"Hey, Jake. Please inform the Finnish police that I have encountered an unknown man who was following me."

"Wow. Hope you are OK. What happened?" Jake asks.

"I'm unharmed but really spooked at the moment. I'm not sure if my meeting was a setup or not at this point," David says. He looks out of the back window of the cab.

"We will talk when you get back to me in a debrief of your encounter," Jake says.

"Sounds good," David says.

David puts his cell phone into his pocket. He sits back in his seat in the cab and momentarily rests. He can feel his heart still pounding from his fast sprint.

His nerves are still on edge as a flashback from the incident at his summer home replays in his mind.

Chapter 7

A Top Secret Sauna

Kallio, Helsinki

On a usually pleasant Nordic summer day, David decides he needs a diversion and walks off the tram after it reaches Kallio. He has spent a whole day working at the United States embassy engaged in drafting cables and responding to calls from United States citizens in need of assistance. David decides to enjoy the weather and walks several blocks past Bear Park, where there are numerous young people sitting at the outdoor café drinking coffee and engaging in conversation.

David thinks it's a good day to experience the communal sauna, where men and women congregate and enjoy the heat and relaxation associated with the sweating culture. The sauna consists of hot, dry heat; a wooden interior; and a small heating element in the corner of the room.

Dave walks inside the sauna club and meets the clerk at the front desk.

"*Terve*. How are you?" Dave announces, proud of the little Finnish he has learned.

"You must be American. You smile way too much and don't look like you are from here," the front desk clerk quips and grins. "What are you doing here in Finland?"

"I'm a bureaucrat. I work at the United States embassy," Dave remarks.

"The new embassy is cool. The Innovation Center at the embassy is beautiful. I like the United States ambassador, Armstrong. He is big into boxing and is a tough guy. However, I heard that during his confirmation hearing before the United States Congress, he did not know anything about Finland. He thought that Finland was a former Communist country," he says.

"I thought that Finns don't go for small talk?" Dave quips. He appears a little confused.

"Yeah, I lived in Canada before. I have changed way too much as a result."

"I will introduce myself then. I am Dave. What is your name?"

"Pekka. Welcome to Finland. Now get the hell out," he chuckles. "We hate foreigners in Helsinki now that there are too many of them living here." Pekka jokingly grins.

"I will remember that during my stay here." David smiles. "Good to meet you, Pekka," he adds and reaches out to shake his hand.

David then walks into the sauna's locker room, changes into his bathing suit, and begins investigating the different types of saunas that the communal sauna has to offer. Some possess dry heat, and others have wet steam. He peers through the sauna windows and sees many of the Finns are sitting wearing towels, trying to brave the heat of the sauna as they sit on a wooden bench. Dave walks into an empty sauna, which consists of a wooden interior, two levels of wooden benches, and a heated unit placed at the far end of the room. There is a bucket that contains water and a scoop sitting on one of the benches. A large wooden thermometer is hanging above the hot sauna. David is hoping to obtain his bearings in the Finnish sauna before sitting with other people. He is sweating a little and takes a scoop of water and throws it in the direction of the heated unit, which results in a direct hit and evaporates into a hot mist that smacks him in the face and causes him to sweat.

A young, very attractive woman in her thirties who possesses light blond hair, blue eyes, and a slim, muscular build enters the sauna and sits down opposite David. She is five-ten, has a button nose, and is wearing a bathing suit. Dave glances at her for several seconds, as she is quite attractive.

There is silence for a moment.

"So, you are David Ivanovich Markoff, I believe?" the women quips in perfect American-accented English.

"How do you know my name?" Dave looks a little nervous and confused.

"I am an officer of the Finnish Security Intelligence Service. We are the security police in Finland. I'm Pia Hejt." She smiles.

"Why meet here?" David questions. He conveys an expression indicating he is a little confused.

"Our meeting must be discreet. In Finland, meeting in the sauna is a normal business practice." Pia pauses a moment to wipe her face with a towel. "We uncovered your name in connection with the investigation into Harri Bergstrom's death. I think we should talk about this at some point. We know your address from the information you submitted on your Finnish visa application, and I tracked you here," Pia says.

"I heard about Harri's death on the radio. Why can't you go through the formal procedures? I'm a diplomat here, after all," David questions.

Pia spouts a knowing smile. "I hope you are here for nice purposes and not working with the CIA without telling us. We have lots of problems with the CIA sending people here without declaring themselves to the SUPO as intelligence officials."

"Honestly, I'm working in the United States Citizen Consular section at the Department of State. The SUPO will have no problems with me," David announces and smiles. "What is the SUPO exactly? I just landed here a couple of weeks ago," David resorts to playing ignorant, which never hurts for dealing with other intelligence services. "Let your opposition tell you what they know is good tradecraft in the intelligence world," David's CIA instructor would preach in class.

"We specialize in security and counter-intelligence here in Finland. The SUPO is similar to the United Kingdom's MI5. In special cases associated with national security, the SUPO leads the police investigation or tracks intelligence targets within the country. We also investigate economic espionage and terrorist threats and fight organized crime," Pia says.

"Why not approach me at the United States embassy for an interview?" David asks. He appears a little puzzled.

"In Finland, the sauna is a relaxed and less menacing place to introduce yourself. We are a friendly organization to the United States. I thought this would be a better avenue to introduce myself here," Pia retorts and smiles.

"Where are you from originally?" Pia asks.

"The Brighton Beach section of Brooklyn in New York City. Do you know where that is?"

"Yes, you must be a Russian speaker, no doubt. I remember there is a large population of Russian speakers living there. I worked as an au pair in New York for an American family for a year. It's an exciting place," Pia remarks.

"I guess you enjoyed lots of partying in Manhattan?" David says and flashes a friendly smile.

"I liked living in Manhattan, but that was a while ago," Pia says.

"Where are you from?" David asks.

"A small town in Finland called Lohja," Pia retorts.

"Where is that exactly?" David asks.

"It's located about thirty minutes west of Helsinki. It's a suburb. There are many Swedish speakers who live there," Pia remarks.

"Pia, I am more than happy to assist with your investigation, but I have to clear my activities with the United States embassy first," David says.

"Thank you. I have to go. Enjoy your sauna." Pia gets up from the sauna's bench and exits the sauna.

Dave grabs his cell phone from his bag, which is lying next to his towel. He makes a call to Jake.

"Hey, it's David. Let's meet. The locals . . . the SUPO have contacted me," David warns.

"No problem. Tomorrow should be best," Jake retorts.

David exits the sauna, walks to the changing room, grabs his things, and walks out of the main door of the communal sauna.

He walks back to his apartment complex. He climbs the stairs to the floor where his apartment is located. He opens his front door and enters his apartment. David takes out his binoculars from his desk drawer and approaches his bedroom window. He scans the streets outside his residence in Kallio. He spots the same black Saab he has seen before and observes that two men are sitting in the front seat and appear to be watching. It's a clear sign of a SUPO surveillance team. David knows that the SUPO follow their targets and track them with efficiency in coordinated teams, which is probably how Pia knew he was in the sauna.

A feeling of both paranoia and anxiety begins to penetrate his body. This all-encompassing feeling immediately brings him back to his time working in Langley, Virginia, when he was an intelligence analyst at the CIA's headquarters.

David remembers long hours involved with his work as a regional analyst. He would sit at his cube drafting assessments for the top United States policy makers. At the time, jogging was David's only solace from the long hours.

David recalls that after a year of passing numerous polygraphs, he finally arrived at the CIA. His first days of work were exciting. He walked into Langley relatively young and unfamiliar with the world of intelligence. He was impressed with the beautiful glass structure of the CIA's headquarters, the number of fantastically painted pictures hanging on the walls, the museums that documented the history and exploits of famous CIA spies, and the highly educated and dedicated employees who worked there. David wanted to prove to everyone that he was a loyal American, and exceling in the intelligence world was his driving motivation for success.

At first, David was assigned to work as South Asia analyst rather than an operations officer. He underwent

CIA training for many weeks to learn the proper techniques of the intelligence profession, better known as *tradecraft*. He attended training, where he was immersed in the CIA's culture and learned the techniques and procedures of being a successful CIA operations officer.

When he returned to CIA headquarters, the atmosphere of the office was collegial. The intelligence analysts supported each other in their efforts to write the best intelligence products for the president and other high-ranking United States government officials. The long hours of writing intelligence reports, attending meetings, and following the latest developments about international politics soon followed. In the middle of all this, David never forgot to jog around the beautiful CIA complex and keep in shape, as he did when he was competing in international triathlons. No matter if he had to work at 5:00 a.m. or 11:00 p.m., David would never forget to run. David enjoyed the competition among analysts, which spilled over to the CIA's yearly unofficial 8K race. This featured a run two times around the road that surrounds the CIA building and encompasses the building complex. The race took place every spring, and David participated in a run with several hundred other analysts and operatives, as hundreds of CIA employees lined up along the route of the runners to cheer. To the surprise of everyone, David won the race, and he felt like he had won a triathlon. He gained the nickname of the "ringer" at the CIA afterwards.

David enjoyed running, but it was more rewarding as he was running with a common goal. He was proud of achieving excellence for his country at the CIA.

Soon thereafter, Russian–US relations turned sour. The FBI arrested dozens of Russian intelligence agents attempting to spy on the United States. As a result, relations between the United States and Russia began to sink into a morass of paranoia and suspicion with the emergence of a new cold war rivalry between the Russian and NATO block countries. David receives a call at his desk one morning. He answers the phone. "Hello. This is Don. I work with the security office. We need to talk about an issue. Can you come to our office?" the security officer on the phone remarks.

"Sure," David says.

David proceeds to walk from his office through a series of endless white hallways to the subterranean level of the CIA complex. He walks into an office marked "Security."

As he arrives at the front desk, David states, "I am looking for Don."

The woman points to the right and remarks, "Down the hallway."

He looks at the cube and finds the one with the nametag marked "Don Edmonds."

David knocks on the cube walls. "I am looking for Don."

"Sit down." Don flashes a polite smile and points to the chair station in front of his desk.

"Is there a problem? How can I assist you?" David remarks.

"Well . . . We hear you speak Russian. Is that right?" Don questions. He opens a file that is lying in front of him on his desk.

"Yes, I speak Russian. That's true," David remarks.

"David, do you have some relatives in Russia or in any other Russian-speaking countries?" Don asks.

"I might. I'm not in contact with any of my relatives. Most of them emigrated from the country following the collapse of the Soviet Union."

"Have you ever visited Russia since your family left the country?" Don inquires.

"No. Is there a problem?" David questions.

"No problem or reason to be worried. We are just engaging in a normal security review. Should we require additional information, we will contact you,"

Don says. He flashes a polite smile. He starts to write in David's file. "Thank you for your time. We will be in touch for any other follow-up," Don adds.

A week after being questioned, David received an email indicating that he would be transferred from his analyst position. Suddenly, David felt like an orphan who was not trusted and was being closely watched. A month later, he received orders that he was to be transferred to Helsinki station, with no career path and no future. In CIA lingo, he had become a "desk sitter." He was now a non-person, who could bide his time on temporary assignments and dreary details teaching at the CIA University.

The loud pounding on the front door of his apartment startles David back to reality. He appears nervous, as he is not expecting anyone. David slowly but quietly approaches his front door. He looks through the door's spy hole and sees nothing. He opens the door. He looks left and right and sees nothing. He looks down and notices an unmarked white envelope lying on the ground. He hesitantly picks the envelope up and carries it inside his apartment. He closes and locks the door. After walking to his kitchen table, he places the envelope down, puts on some gloves, and takes a knife out of his drawer. David carefully opens the white envelope. David finds a small piece of paper with pasted letters. It states in Russian Cyrillic letters, "Are you friend or foe? Your actions will tell. We regret the death of Terhi. Siloviki."

David is shocked and confused. He begins to breathe heavily. Many questions go through his mind: *Who are the Siloviki? What do they want with me? Why are they not contacting me directly? Did they kill Terhi?*

Chapter 8

Day 30 of Jaanika's Detention

Minsk, Belarus

Jaanika sits in her small cell staring at the wall. She is sweating and suffering from the heat, as her brain feels like its boiling inside. Her gaze is momentarily focused on a huge rat, which scurries into her small cell and begins foraging for food. Jaanika begins to sing to herself. It's an Estonian melody that her mother taught her in her youth; it was banned during the Soviet occupation but was sung as resistance for pro-independence Estonians. The words emerge from Jaanika's soul as she sings and hums. The lyrics echo along the corridors of the KGB detention center. This provides her with courage to face her jailers.

While Jaanika sings, she hears the distant sound of approaching footsteps, which become louder and louder as an unseen person walks down the hallway. An unidentified man wearing a black mask walks into the corridor from out of the shadows. He is five feet, four inches tall and wears a gray uniform. He grabs the keys and opens the cell door.

"Come," the man demands in thickly accented English.

Jaanika slowly rises from the floor of the cell and struggles to get to her feet. The man in black puts handcuffs on her wrists and stretches her arms all the way back to the point of absolute pain. Jaanika limps a little as she walks down the hallway. She appears emaciated, and her face looks worn and dirty. The echo of the screams of an unknown individual can be heard as she slowly progresses down the hallway. The guard walks behind her. After several minutes of limping down the hallway, Jaanika arrives at a small room and spies a table and two chairs.

"Sit down," the guard orders and slams the door shut. Jaanika proceeds to take a seat. Another man in black walks into the room along with Ivan.

"Jaanika, how are you feeling?" Ivan states and places a bottle containing a soft drink next to her on the table. Both men sit across the table from Jaanika.

"We need some information from you. Who were the people involved with you in the flight over Minsk?" Ivan questions. He flashes an imposingly stern expression.

"I don't know what you're talking about," Jaanika responds in protest. She shakes her head and sits back in her chair.

"OK, tell me, why were you visiting Belarus?" Ivan adds in a stern tone.

"I was in Belarus as a tourist. Why don't you believe me?" Jaanika pleads. She sits back in her chair and flashes an exasperated expression.

"Jaanika Olson. We know you're Estonian and American. What were you doing in Belarus?" Ivan remarks. He points at Jaanika with his right finger.

"Tourism," Jaanika says and begins to weep violently. Tears pour from her eyes. She rubs her eyes with her hands, and her body begins to shake.

"Do you work for the CIA?" Ivan questions while looking directly at her with a menacing stare.

Jaanika does not respond. For a moment, there is silence in the room. "Listen, I can only ask you questions, but my friend is less friendly. He will demand answers. I think you know what that means, Jaanika." Ivan looks at the masked guard sitting behind him.

"Jaanika, the choice is yours," Ivan says. He rocks his head back and forth in frustration.

Ivan leaves the room and hears Jaanika scream as he closes the interrogation room door. He walks down the hallway and receives a call on his cell. He takes the cell out of his pocket, recognizes it as his commanding officer Valerie, and answers the call.

"Yes, sir," Ivan answers.

"How is the operation in Finland proceeding?" Valerie questions.

"Fine. I am about to meet with a person who will be joining me on the mission. He is a good man," Ivan adds.

"Good luck, Ivan. I will inform you about the details of our previous discussion."

"Yes, sir." Ivan remarks and puts the phone in his pocket.

Ivan enters his gray, Russian-built car and drives outside Minsk to a government facility that contains a shooting range.

He engages in target shooting and then runs the obstacle course. After several hours, he walks to the locker room and enters a classroom with about ten students in attendance.

He interrupts the class. "I would like to see Vladimir Serkin."

He stands up in the class. "Please come with me, as I want to talk to you," Ivan orders.

"Yes, sir." A young man in his twenties stands up and salutes.

Ivan looks at Vladimir and then walks him to a room, where they both sit down.

"Listen, Vladimir. I see you're the top of your class in training," Ivan remarks.

"Yes, sir," Vladimir responds.

"We have a mission that is very dangerous. I need the best man for this. How would you like to be working for me?" Ivan questions.

"The mission sounds good," Vladimir states. He looks enthusiastic.

"This is a secret mission. Do not mention anything to anyone about this. Do you have any questions?" Ivan asks.

"When will we be leaving?" Vladimir questions.

"Soon. I think we will make a good team." Ivan smiles a little.

"You will receive your orders in the next week. You are dismissed," Ivan remarks.

Vladimir gets up from his seat, salutes, walks out of the room, and returns to his class.

Ivan sits at his desk and plans the next operation.

Chapter 9

A Clandestine Source

David walks into the United States embassy and enters his cubicle in the Consular Affairs section. He sits at his desk, logs onto his computer, and begins to read the emails he has received in his inbox.

At lunch, he makes sure he is not being watched by anyone. He proceeds to walk up to the Security Office. He walks through the door and then enters the code that allows him to enter a secure room. He opens it and sees Jake typing away at his desk with an ice hockey poster hanging prominently on his desk wall.

"Hey! However are you doing? How did Helsinki's ice hockey team do last night?" David asks. He flashes a polite smile.

"I'm good. The team did well, too. They won for a change. I'm not sure you know, but the team was just bought by one of President Vladimirovich minions, and he has brought very talented ice hockey players to play in Helsinki," Jake says. "Are you a hockey fan? I know that ice hockey is the Russian tradition," Jake asks.

"My father was a big Soviet Red Army team fan. I like ice hockey but became a runner and triathlete, to the dismay of my father."

David takes a seat next to Jake's desk. "I came here during my lunch break to file a foreign intelligence contact report. I phoned you about it previously. I want to tell you that the locals, the Finnish SUPO, have made contact with me about the death of Harri in Helsinki."

"Where was this?" Jake questions. He appears a little concerned.

"In Kallio at a communal sauna. I think the SUPO agent obtained my address from my Finnish visa application and just followed me from there. She wants an interview. I played dumb and will continue to if she interviews me again," David says.

"Pretty brazen. The SUPO must be aggressively engaging in counter intelligence in Helsinki due to the increased Russian threat in the country," Jake says. "Do you think the SUPO knows you're working for the CIA?" Jake asks.

"I think they suspect I am, but I'm not certain. The SUPO might be watching me sporadically. I have not seen any sign of surveillance in the last couple weeks," David says. "By the way, I received another note under my door. It was again from the 'Siloviki.' The note stated that they know who I am and appear to be monitoring me. I speak Russian fluently and know Soliviki is a Russian word that describes the Russian elite in Valdimirovich's government who possess a background in intelligence, having worked for the Soviet KGB or the Russian SVR, GRU, or FSB," David informs.

"I have never heard of the group," Jake says. He appears a little perplexed. "Check our computer system, and see if we possess any information or cable traffic about them," he adds.

"David, let me know how well the interview goes when the SUPO talks to you at the embassy. I have another operational task for you to do. I need you to work as a handler for a good source that I have been running in the past. He is your asset now. His name is Jose Augusto Lopez, and his source name is AMERICANO. He is fairly high ranking in the MC Raging Angels here, which is one of the more notorious biker gangs in Finland. You may not know, but Finland imports American criminals here for the crime scene. AMERICANO possesses good intelligence. Go through the system, review our last contacts, talk to him, and come back with a report. Be careful, as these bikers are pretty nasty folks. They are associated with narcotics smuggling, prostitution, and human trafficking. Remember one rule of being a handler. Doubt is the most important characteristic to possess in your job. Half of what he tells you will be lies, and the other half may be the truth. You have to determine what's the truth. Also, I will give you a packet of euros. Don't forget to get his signature when you give it to him," Jake mentions.

"How would you characterize AMERICANO as a source?" David asks.

"He is a good access to human trafficking, drugs, and some intelligence activities and possesses a fairly reliable reporting history," Jake says.

"Thanks for the assignment. It will be a break from the boredom of United States passport issues, and I can use my operation skills," David says.

David sits down, drafts his report, and sends it. ***Operations Cable Helsinki Station to CIA Headquarters, SUPO Contact Report,*** *Limited dissemination, Directorate of Operations, Europe Desk: I have been contacted by Pia Hjelt, a presumed officer of the Finnish Intelligence Security Service. I encountered her in a communal sauna in Kallio. I'm unsure if she could be a potential CIA source in the future but may follow up to see if she may assist the agency. I am available for any additional follow-up tasks to fill information gaps.* He walks out of his office and returns to his desk in the Consular Section Office.

At 5:00 p.m., David leaves his office. He drops by a public bathroom. He takes out his bag and changes his clothes. He puts on a fake beard and long hair as a disguise. He is hoping to blend in with the biker crowd. He proceeds to catch a tram headed north to Pasila, which is a section of town that contains mostly immigrant housing, low-income Soviet-designed complexes, and where biker gangs predominate.

David sits in the back of the tram looking for any indication that the SUPO are watching him. It could be a passenger looking out of place heading to Pasila, someone whom he might have spotted before, or any person involved in anything out of the ordinary. David spots no surveillance and exits the tram. He walks several blocks to an establishment known as Metal Barri. It looks like a typical heavy metal dive bar, which includes a dartboard, an American confederate and Finnish flag, and tough, tattooed men wearing leather jackets that have biker club insignia emblazoned on the back. David is struck by the heavy metal music playing loudly in the background as he approaches the establishment. He walks inside and then sits down at a table located in the corner. David puts on a New York baseball cap, with which AMERICANO will be able to identify him as the person to meet.

David sits quietly, being careful to make no eye contact with anyone inside the bar. He is startled by the sensation of a hand touching his left shoulder. He worriedly looks back and spies a burly man in his thirties with multiple tattoos and massive hair. The man flashes a big grin.

David uses the contact words. *"Tu madre vive en Texas?"*

Lopez responds, "No, she lives in Lapland."

"How are you doing, motherfucker?" Lopez smiles and laughs. He then sits down at the table in a chair situated opposite David.

"Good. Any sign of the police?" David remarks. He scans the bar nervously.

"No, they are easy to avoid here. I'm more worried about other biker gang members. We have a number of them in Helsinki. It's getting crowded now in Finland. I remember when we were the first ones here in the 1990s," Lopez remarks. He smiles menacingly.

"I will be your new handler. I hear you're good at reporting on human trafficking. So, can you provide me with any information about movements into and out of Finland that strike you as unusual at the moment?" David asks.

Lopez thinks for a moment. "Yeah, now that you ask. I remember that we were contacted by some

Russian-speaking guys to assist in obtaining weapons and a safe house for a hit," Lopez says.

"Any idea the target of the hit maybe?" David asks.

"No information yet. The people we are in contact with seem unusual. Most hits are biker, Somali gang, or Serbian types. This guy seemed very professional. This is very unusual for Finland," Lopez states.

"I have to follow up on a past tasking. Do you have the information from the laptop of the Somali-Finnish Islamist Al-Shabab supporter that we had requested from you?" David inquires.

"Here it is. This was an easy piece of information to steal." Lopez passes the thumb drive across the table to David.

"Thanks. Please follow up on the hit for me," David orders. He takes the thumb drive and places it safely within his pocket. "I have several other tasks for you. I have written these on the paper. The first priority is information about the potential assassin," David adds.

David reaches into his pocket and passes a wad of money inside an envelope to Lopez. He gives him a piece of paper. "Please sign this." David points to the place on the piece of paper for Lopez to sign. He takes out a pen from his pocket and gives it to Lopez.

"Thanks." Lopez signs the document with the pen and then grins.

"I'm just wondering. How did you end up in Finland?" David questions. He places the signed paper securely into his pocket.

"*Mi amigo*. It was fucking destiny. *Mi bonita* Finnish *chica*—my girlfriend—and I met in Texas, and she dragged me here in the 1990s. I arrived here and took advantage of the cash opportunities that were less available in the United States for outlaw biker *one percenters* like myself. Plus, the Finnish government subsidizes our biker club. I love fucking Finnish social democracy." Lopez smiles slyly and chuckles a little.

"*One percenters*? What is that exactly?" David asks. He appears a little confused.

"One percenters. We are the ones who commit 90 percent of the crimes in the United States. We are proud of this fact as outlaw bikers," Lopez says.

A big, burly man walks into the bar wearing an outlaw biker jacket. He possesses tattoos all over his neck and has long hair hanging down to his shoulders. He glances around the bar. David notices his actions. The dark-haired man, who appears to be in his thirties, takes out a sawed-off shotgun from beneath his jacket and starts brandishing it. "You fucking pricks. You killed my brother!" the biker yells in Finnish as if possessed and seeking revenge. His face is red, and he flashes a sinister smile. He randomly begins aiming and then shooting at people within the bar.

The bangs of the shotgun blast ring out loudly. The smell of gunpowder fills the air of the small, dingy bar. A man wearing a biker jacket falls down from his chair and appears wounded. A loud bang of another gunshot follows shortly. David reacts quickly, diving under the table for cover. Lopez quickly joins him. The loud moans of the injured can be heard in the bar.

"*Vittu!* That asshole," Lopez whispers. He is crouching under the table seeking cover and carefully observing the unhinged biker.

Dave hears the loud bangs of additional gunshots and the clicks revealing the reloading of a shotgun. "*Vittu!*" the unhinged biker screams. He shoots, reloads, and begins to walk from table to table looking for more people to kill.

David crouches under the table and observes that the gunman is momentarily distracted while he is attempting to search for ammunition to reload his weapon. He springs up from under the table and sprints out the doorway. David glances back for a moment and sees Lopez running behind him. He also spots the gunman walking outside the bar following him. The gunman cocks the rifle, aims, and takes two shots. David sprints forward with his arms pumping desperately. Lopez follows David, as he is running fast behind him. The loud bang of a rifle blast rings out within David's ears, but it's clear the shots have missed their mark.

David glances behind him, and the gunman appears to reload and aims his sights on David. The gunman appears startled by the sounds of the sirens of fast-approaching Finnish police cars. He lowers his gun and runs away as fast as he can in the opposite direction.

David continues to sprint through an alleyway and over another a fence. He is breathing hard. He dives behind some trash cans, sits down momentarily, checks his pocket, and finds that he still has the thumb drive that Lopez gave to him. He feels lucky to be alive.

Chapter 10

A Midnight Run in Helsinki

It's 11:00 p.m. in Helsinki. Tens of thousands of runners line up to race through the middle of the city for the famous Midnight Run. The landmark Orthodox Church is lit up in Finland's national colors of blue and white, giving a mystical feel to the event. David is lined up at the start with the thousands of runners for the famous 10K race that passes through central Helsinki. He is wearing his fashionable blue-and-white running pants. The weather is an unusually pleasant sixty degrees. David readies himself. He begins his last-minute check of water, which is attached to a belt that is hanging from his hip. He checks his running shoes, which appear in order, and begins to stretch his hamstrings in preparation for the race.

Midnight arrives. A loud horn sounds, which signals the start. David accelerates from a fast trot and begins to run at a seven-minute-mile pace through Helsinki. His arms push forward with every step as he continues to speed up. After several minutes, he starts to sprint at a comfortable pace. He wears headphones and has his smart phone is strapped to his arm. He runs along in a crowded path of runners that takes him on a route that follows the Baltic Sea, continues around Helsinki Parkland, and passes through the financial district. David looks around, as other Finns are running briskly around him, and suddenly spies Pia within the crowd of runners. She is wearing a blue shirt and shorts with a Finnish flag imprinted on them. She sees David, waves, and motions for him to run alongside her.

David runs in her direction while keeping up his running pace. He is sweating now and breathing heavily with every stride. David runs alongside Pia. "*Terve*, Pia. How are you feeling?" Dave questions.

"Great. I love this race. Everyone living in Helsinki seems to be running or watching the race. Most Finns are usually in the countryside or Spain during the summer months. It's a midnight party of runners," Pia remarks. She smiles happily.

"What inspired you to decide to run this road race?" Dave inquires between breaths.

"The SUPO sponsors a number of people to participate. We are required to be in good physical condition. This is normal for a police organization. What about you?" Pia questions as she continues running at a fast pace. She appears quite interested in the answer.

"Running keeps me in shape and out of trouble, which is a big bonus. I would run while living in Kenya. The marines would hit the local brothels. As a single man, I would refrain from going to the brothels and getting sexual diseases by occupying my time running. I was a triathlete at one point," David says.

"That is very ethical of you. I am beginning to respect you despite the fact that you're an American bureaucrat." Pia smiles warmly and continues to run.

"So what is your story? Why police and intelligence work?" David questions. He continues to jog.

"Well, my father was a police officer. I guess I'm following the family tradition. And you?" Pia asks.

"I think I'm running away from things, mostly. I was working at a law firm. I applied for a job on a government website. I was hoping that the United States government could be a nice place to disappear," David says. He smiles and takes out a bottle of water he has strapped to his belt. He puts it to his lips and drinks.

"How do you like living in Kallio? It's a left-wing, hipster, sauna-loving, and café lovers' paradise," Pia asks.

"It's nice. I lived in Brooklyn. It kind of reminds me of the Williamsburg section of the borough, but with lots of less crazy people and even less small talk. The massage parlors that predominate Kallio are also a big difference from Brooklyn," David says. He chuckles.

"So, will I see you in the sauna again? It was not a bad visit in my aesthetic opinion. You are very good-looking is what I am hinting at here," David quips. He spouts a friendly grin.

"Another officer will come over to interview you later. I would not mind seeing you again, though. Maybe we can meet in Kallio under nicer circumstances," Pia adds.

"Sure. You already have my email and other detailed information." David smiles slyly while running.

"*Joo*," Pia adds.

"I will see you later, then. I don't want to keep you from running with your fellow SUPO runners," David says.

"*Hei Hei!* I will see you at the end of the race," Pia says.

David sprints away from Pia. After twenty minutes, he approaches the finish line. David checks his time on his smartphone to see that he has completed the race at a 7:30-per-mile pace. It seems to David that all of Helsinki is lined up near the end of the race cheering the runners on at the completion of the race, despite the fact that it is the middle of the night.

David crosses the finish line, takes a cup of water, and looks for his bag, which has been transported to the bag-holding area and contains a towel and a change of clothes. David begins to cool down by engaging in stretches. He again spies Pia, who appears to have crossed the finish line several minutes before. He slowly walks over to where other runners, who have completed the race, are also standing.

David looks at Pia. "You look in great shape. I guess police officers don't eat donuts in Finland."

"Kiitos," Pia says. He spouts a friendly smile.

"What are you doing after this?" David questions.

"I'm not sure yet. Maybe I will go to sleep," Pia says.

"Why not join me for a coffee in Kallio? I promise no jokes about policemen or Sweden," David quips.

"How can I resist?" Pia says.

David and Pia walk away from the finish line and search for a cab. David hails a cab and takes it to Kallio. Arriving near his apartment, he sees that Kallio is packed and teaming with partygoers. Pia and David exit the backseat of the cab, pay the fare, walk to Helsinki Barri, and sit down. The place is typical Kallio, which contains unusual fixtures, micro-brewed beers, and a vegetarian menu.

"So you're one of the SUPO's finest," David remarks. He takes a sip from a water bottle lying on the table.

"Yes, I am proud to be a part of the organization. We have a unique history and tradition here in Finland, though not the budget your FBI and CIA possess," Pia says.

"Are all the agents in the SUPO as good-looking as you?" David inquires. He smiles.

"Thanks for the compliment. Though I know you Americans excel in small talk and are not necessarily sincere. So, why Finland of all places and working for the United States government?" Pia asks.

"I feel like I am being analyzed by you, Pia. Well, my deceased wife was from Finland, and I was transferred here from Washington DC. I do have many other hidden talents also," David says.

"What else could there be?" Pia remarks. She looks quite interested.

"You're going to have to use your investigative skills to find out." David smiles. He takes another sip from his water bottle.

"My place is down the street. Might you join me?" David adds.

Pia looks at David, and they kiss. She smiles at him. "The offer is tempting, but I will have to call you later," Pia remarks.

Pia kisses David again and smiles at him. "I think you're a good kisser at least. I will be in touch with you, but I really have to go now," Pia adds.

"Coming from a SUPO member, I think I should be a little scared by your statement." David grins.

Pia gets up from the table and exits the bar. David receives an email on his smart phone. He feels a little worried. He knows that he should report his encounter with Pia, as she works for a foreign intelligence organization. He decides that reporting the contact might jeopardize his already precarious situation working for the CIA.

David looks at his smartphone and spots an encrypted email. He opens it. It reads: *Let's schedule a drop. Mi amigo.*

David walks several blocks to his apartment. He opens the door to the apartment to find the top latch slightly unhinged. A chill goes down his spine. *Am I paranoid?* David asks himself. He slowly opens the door. All is dark. He switches on the light. He sees his computer sitting on the desk unmolested. He looks through his papers to see if anything is missing and does not find anything disturbed or out of place.

A man, who is dressed in black, bolts out of the kitchen, pushes David to the side of the desk, and runs out the door. David is startled. He loses his balance and falls to the ground. He quickly gets up, grabs his handgun from his desk, and runs out of his apartment in hot pursuit of the intruder. He follows the sounds of the man's footsteps and sees he is running down the apartment stairway. David opens the stairway door and descends the staircase. He peers down it. As David descends, he spots a six-feet-tall male in his twenties who is dressed in black and running fast. The intruder exits the bottom of the apartment stairway, bolts out the door of the apartment building, and runs through a series of alleys that divide several apartments. David reaches the exit and sees the intruder running down an alleyway. David follows him in relentless pursuit.

The man runs through alleyways for five blocks and then turns right onto the main road. David speeds up and gets closer to the man. The man stops for a moment. He turns toward David, raises his hand, which contains a handgun, and fires several shots at

David. The loud cracks of the gun echo in the distance. David hears the whistle of bullets passing close to his ear. His heart is pumping rapidly, and adrenaline streams through his veins.

David quickly draws his pistol, aims, and takes four shots at the man. The pops of the gun loudly crack the air as they leave his barrel. The sound rings in David's ears.

The intruder, who is wearing black, drops down on his knee for a second. He appears to have been shot in his leg. He stops momentarily and winces in pain. The man limps forward toward an intersection.

David rapidly runs toward the man. A loud screech of wheels can be heard rapidly approaching the intruder, who is limping at the intersection. A black BMW appears to be speeding. The car stops, the man looks at David, gives him the middle finger, and jumps inside the front seat of the car. The BMW speeds away.

David looks a little dumbfounded as to what has just occurred. He makes a call on his cell phone to Jake. The phone rings.

"What's up?" Jake remarks.

"Someone broke into my apartment. I chased him, but he shot at me and managed to escape," David reports. He sounds a little winded on the phone.

"Are you OK?" Jake asks.

"I'm unharmed," David reports.

"Can you identify the person or know what organization he may be affiliated with?" Jake asks.

"He was clad in black. He might have been associated with the Siloviki. That is all that I can say," David states.

"I can get someone to come to your place and attempt to collect evidence. I will call the local police. Glad you're safe at least. Keep well," Jake remarks.

"Thanks," David states.

David sits on the sidewalk in the middle of Kallio. He feels stunned. He wonders, *Who is seeking to kill me? What were they looking for inside my apartment? And are they connected to Terhi's death?*

Chapter 11

Jaanika's Gulag

The moldy white walls of the interrogation room seem both claustrophobic and dull. Jaanika sits in the chair at the end of a white table, seemingly alone in the world.

A tall, Slavic-looking man enters the room and possesses a dour expression and surly manner. He reaches to the chair, grabs it, and throws it at Jaanika. It flies through the air, hits the wall with a loud crack and bang, and barely misses Jaanika's head. "Do you deny helping the teddy bear bombers and the CIA?" he yells.

Jaanika flashes a smirk. "I have told you this before during the last interrogation. I was here visiting Belarus as a tourist."

"You are lying again, Jaanika. You bitch!" the Slavic man yells. He takes his right hand and violently connects it with Jaanika's cheek. Jaanika recoils in pain. She touches her hand to her face, where a bruise appears.

"I am not lying," Jaanika protests.

"You are a spy for the Finnish SUPO!" the man yells. He cocks his right hand into a fist, recoils it, and violently lands a punch that impacts Jaanika's stomach. Jaanika recoils in pain again. She appears disoriented for a moment and regains her composure.

"You don't want to hear me!" Jaanika remarks.

"I am done with you!" the man yells again and exits the room.

A female guard walks into the room. "You come!" she orders.

Jaanika rises from her chair. The guard opens the door to the interrogation room. Jaanika proceeds to slowly hobble down the dimly lit hallway. Jaanika sings to herself in a beautiful Estonian melody. She slowly walks near a window. She stops for moment and looks outside. Jaanika views the sun and a recreation yard, where some inmates are walking around close to a high perimeter wall.

The Nordic summer sun, Jaanika thinks to herself. She smiles for moment and remembers her life in Helsinki.

"Come!" the woman prison guard yells.

Jaanika starts walking again and approaches her cell. The guard opens it. She enters, and the guard locks the jail cell.

Jaanika observes that no one is watching. She reaches over to her cell's wall and slowly takes out some loose plaster. She reaches inside and inspects the sharp implements that she has cobbled together.

Jaanika begins singing to herself in Estonian, almost weeping, and falls asleep. When she opens her eyes, she gets up from her bed and starts to stretch. Everything in the prison is pitch black. It appears to be the middle of the night.

Jaanika notices the bars to her cell look a little different. She investigates and finds that the jail cell is now unlocked. *This is a confusing development,* Jaanika thinks to herself.

She looks around and does not see any guards. Jaanika takes several of her tools from the hiding place within her cell and quickly starts to walk down the hallway. She sees a guard approaching. She stops and momentarily hides in a corner. The guard passes by her. Jaanika looks both ways and continues undetected.

She begins to sprint with every ounce of energy that she can muster. She passes through several hallways, arriving at a door that leads to the recreation area of the prison. She quickly pulls all her tools out of her pocket. She takes a small, pointed tool that she has crafted and places it inside the lock. She spends several minutes trying to pick the lock and manages to open the latch. The door opens, and Jaanika walks out of the yard, which is deserted. The outside is pitch black, except for the lights of the guard towers above.

She slowly crouches down inside the gate and warily looks right and left for anyone who may be watching. There are small video cameras everywhere, and the wall of the prison is several meters away in the darkness. Jaanika waits and prepares for her break to freedom.

Jaanika takes several elongated pin-like pieces of rock, which possess sharp edges on the ends. She has a small rock in hand and appears to be ready for her final escape to freedom. Jaanika unleashes a burst of speed and sprints as if possessed by another force. She approaches the prison's wall and begins to use her tools to drill spikes in the bricks within the wall, which allow her to climb the tall edifice. As quickly as she can, she bangs the homemade spikes into the concrete, places her foot on each spike to lift her up, and then uses the rock to force new spikes into the wall above her. She rises from the ground at a rapid rate and appears unnoticed by the guards in the distant towers.

An alarm suddenly sounds inside the prison. Jaanika panics. She quickly climbs to the top of the prison wall and is able to bypass the small razor wire lining the top of the wall. She then jumps down to the ground and is immediately confronted by a young armed guard. Both appear surprised by each other's sudden appearance.

Jaanika quickly spins around, lifts her left leg in the air, and connects her right leg with the man's stomach with full force. The resulting blow knocks the man to the ground. She runs in the opposite direction from the guard. The loud pops and echo of gunfire coming in front of Jaanika frighten her.

"Halt or you will be killed," the guard yells in the distance in front of Jaanika.

Jaanika stops in her tracks as she spots three men. They all possess automatic weapons, which are pointed at her. She raises her hands and surrenders.

One of the men laughs. "We knew you would be stupid enough to attempt to escape. Now we can add that to the charges against you. You will never leave here."

The three men begin to swarm Jaanika and engage in repeated kicks to her side. Jaanika falls to the ground. She winces in pain as she absorbs the numerous blows to her side and back.

Chapter 12

A Party of Spies

From the outside located in the Kaivopuisto, the exterior of the United States embassy in Helsinki glows softly from a translucent textured glass façade that is black-lit. The building is perched next to the Baltic Sea, within a sea of birch trees, and appears to mimic the shape of a sail.

Inside the embassy, David hears the distant echo of small talk and conversation within the modernist structure as he walks from his office into the central hall to join an international diplomatic Finnish–American celebration. In the distance, David catches the music of famous Finnish classical composer Jean Sibelius echoing and quietly filling the room. David saunters into the room wearing a suit and tie. He spots many United States and foreign diplomats mixing and mingling and notices that the main hall is inspiring and serene as natural light and wooden materials blend to create a unique experience. He looks up and sees a wooden, white sculpture that is suspended from the ceiling. David looks down and immediately spots the United States ambassador, Cliff Armstrong, in attendance. Cliff is sporting his tuxedo along with his signature grin.

Ambassador Armstrong spots David and walks up to him. "David, good to see you again," the ambassador says. He extends his hand for a shake.

"Nice to see you also," David responds, firmly shaking his hand. He flashes a polite, businesslike smile. The ambassador walks to the next person to talk to.

Jake walks into the party and is prominently wearing an emblem from Minnesota's professional ice hockey team on his lapel, along with a tie and suit. He approaches David. "Nice to see you have dressed up and look sharp!" He chuckles a little and grins.

"Your Minnesota nice is showing! Glad you support the Nordic Stars, even while living in Finland." David flashes a friendly smile.

"Did you hear that we may have a prestigious guest in attendance tonight?" Jake says. He smiles slyly.

"Who's that? A famous guest would not be caught dead in Helsinki during good weather in the summer. I think they would be spending time at their summer home or at one of the numerous festivals taking place in the countryside," David says. He looks around the room trying to spot the famous guest and does not recognize anyone.

"David, you will see shortly. It's highly classified. I have to engage in more small talk. Hope you enjoy the party," Jake says. He walks away from David and in the direction of the United States ambassador.

In walks Finnish Prime Minister Tarja Manninen into the celebration. She possesses red hair, is wearing a red blazer, a black shirt, and a fashionable necklace. The prime minister greets the United States ambassador and high-ranking members of the Department of State.

David appears quite surprised by Tarja's presence. After a couple of minutes, Tarja walks over to David. "Good to meet you." She extends her hand for a shake.

"Good to meet you also, Prime Minister," David remarks. He shakes her hand firmly.

"The United States ambassador mentioned your name and said you're a Russian expert," Tarja says.

"I appreciate the ambassador's compliments, but I think you Finns know the Russians best. I was born in Vyborg, Russia, and my family is ethnic Russian, but we left the country long ago. I have been living in New York City and Washington DC and only moved here recently. DC is a city that distorts your worldview by overexposure to electronic slide presentations, think tank reports, and the delusional insight that writing emails represents progress of sorts. I think Finland's memories of two wars with the Soviet Union likely provides a better analysis than one I can provide," David remarks. He displays a serious expression.

Tarja replies diplomatically, "You are humble. Finland's years of dealing with the Russians as tourists to Lappeenranta and Helsinki or customers to sell expensive pizza to in Lapland has made us soft. Only time will tell. It was good meeting you, though." She walks away with her aide following behind her and heading in the direction of the United States ambassador.

David is startled as another man approaches him. "I'm Yuri." A well-dressed man with bushy eyebrows and Slavic features, who is sporting a demure smile and blue suit and tie, effortlessly takes out his business card and launches it into the air, which results in a mesmerizing flight and precise landing into the center of David's shirt pocket. David's facial expression reveals he is quite impressed by Yuri's trick. He reaches into his shirt pocket and retrieves the card. He momentarily views it. It states, "Yuri Domerov. Second Secretary of the Russian Embassy Finland, Embassy of the Russian Federation."

"Nice to meet you. Have you been to Russia lately?" Yuri inquires. He extends his hand for a shake.

David shakes his hand. "No, I have been too busy in Helsinki, unfortunately," David says.

"You should go. Russians like Americans. It's the United States government that's the problem currently. So, what do you do at the United States embassy? Wait, if it's a secret, don't tell me," Yuri replies. He puts his hand out to accentuate his point.

David pauses for a minute. He smiles politely. "I have no secrets to hide from the Russians. I just work at the United States embassy in the United States Citizen section of the Consular Division. My family is from Karelia, so I have to visit Russia at some point," David says.

"If you travel to Russia, give me a call. I will assist you in any way I can. Your family is Russian, so you must visit. Call me," Yuri says. He flashes a friendly smile.

"It was good to meet you. Thanks for the offer." David flashes a diplomatic smile and shakes his hand. David surmises that Yuri must be a Russian Sluzhba Vneshney Razvedski (SVR) intelligence agent. The card flip is a sign of a true intelligence professional who can recruit sources. David knows the card flip is good tradecraft.

David walks out of the room and onto a beautiful balcony that overlooks the Baltic Sea. The midnight sun is perched on top of the sky at 10 p.m. Distant ships can be viewed traversing the Baltic Sea. A woman approaches David from behind and taps him on his back. "So, you are David Markoff?"

David turns around. "Yes, that's me. How do you know who I am?" David inquires. He seems a little startled by her approach. He sees an extremely tense-looking, middle-aged woman who possesses blond hair and blue eyes and is dressed in contemporary French style. "Before I tell you some important information, I think you should know that I'm working for the European Union Delegation as a liaison. I work for the European Union's INTCEN, which analyzes intelligence. We are the EU's intelligence agency. It's based in Brussels." She pauses for a moment and whispers, "I want you to know that I heard about the attempt on your life. I feel so sorry for you and your deceased wife. My name is Greta, by the way."

David appears a little puzzled. "Thank you, Greta, but . . . how exactly did you learn about what happened to me?" David inquires.

Greta looks around the room and whispers, "Well, I have my own sources, which I can't disclose to you. Listen, I wanted to warn you. The people who you think are your friends are targeting you. My sources know what happened to you at your summer home." She pauses. She worriedly scans the room to see if anyone is listening.

"What do you know exactly? Who are your sources?" David inquires. He appears quite concerned.

Greta whispers, "I know enough that I can't tell you anymore information or my life will be in jeopardy. You must work for United States intelligence. Sorry to rush, but I have to get back to the reception." She walks away from David and disappears into the party.

David feels dumbstruck by Greta's revelations. A chill goes down his spine, and a feeling of paranoia overcomes him. He wonders what Greta's motives for telling him are and if she is telling the truth. He stares at the Baltic Sea for a moment and ponders his situation. David thinks, *Who is my friend, and who is my enemy?*

Chapter 13

A Friendly Foreign Intelligence Service

"There is nothing more dangerous than an intelligence operative from a friendly foreign intelligence agency like the United Kingdom's MI6 or, in this case, the Israeli MOSSAD," Jake remarks sitting next to David inside a secret room at the United States embassy.

"Why do you think that is exactly? I think the Islamic State is pretty dangerous now. I never heard of a friendly intelligence agency chopping heads off of people," David asks. He appears a little puzzled sitting at his desk, which is positioned opposite Jake's.

"David, as you know, all spies want to collect intelligence. A friendly intelligence organization will be provided with information and attempt to obtain more information from you in a cunning way. After all, that is the nature of any good intelligence agency. Please be careful about what you state to them. They love to trick you into revealing more information than we want to share. If you appear as dumb as possible, you will have no problems. You should act friendly, though. This is all a game, and no need not to be polite," Jake advises.

"So, why are we working with the Israelis on this operation exactly?" David asks.

"Listen, your source, TEHRAN EXILE, provided threat information about a possible Hezbollah operative. As you know, the SUPO obeys the law too much. We need someone to break into the apartment and search for evidence, such as pocket litter, links to other possible operatives, and any evidence of casing of possible targets. It's all plausible deniability. The Israelis excel at this, and they are willing to work with us during this operation, as there is a possible threat to their interests in Finland also," Jake says.

"What is the game plan for this operation?" David asks.

"You and an Israeli operative, code name DANNY, will meet at the Helsinki University city center campus. You will meet the MOSSAD agent and assist their operative as they case out the target's apartment. You will then enter and see what we can find out about the Iranian target. Come back with a good report. I know HQ would like to know the fruits of our joint operations. It makes good talking points to the director at his daily operations brief," Jake informs.

"Got it." David smiles.

David walks out of the embassy several hours later. He returns to his apartment and changes into street attire. He proceeds to the tram stop and takes a tram, which travels from Kallio to east Helsinki. He arrives wearing jeans and a white shirt, and he carries a backpack full of materials to carry out the operation; this includes all tools required to break into the apartment and retrieve electronic file information.

David arrives outside the Uusi Café, which is located near Helsinki University center. He is careful to observe any possible surveillance by the SUPO. He looks 360 degrees and sees no overt cameras; he looks left and right and observes no street cleaners. He scans the area for any possible unidentified police cars. David peers above him and observes nothing unusual, such as drones. He is confident that he engaged in a diligent surveillance sweep. David proceeds to enter the café and sits down.

A man wearing a baseball cap walks up to him. "Hey, I remember you from New York." He sports a huge smile and sits down next to David.

"Nice to see you again," David says. He smiles politely.

"It's so good to see you again also. Are you ready for the party?" The Israeli agent says. He smiles slyly.

"Sure, I love parties," David says.

"Walk with me, and I will take you to the event," the Israeli agent says. He gets up from the table and proceeds to lead David in the direction of a white van.

"This is our transport," the Israeli agent proclaims. He nonverbally points in the direction of the van.

The Israeli agent opens the driver's seat door, and David enters the white van, which contains the words "*Valtonen Oy*" printed on the side with large letters. The van moves forward and travels from east Helsinki to Pasila. They arrive near a small apartment complex. Both David and DANNY walk to the back of the van. DANNY opens a box that contains uniforms.

"This will be our disguise. I think it will fit you nicely." He throws the garment over to David.

David swiftly receives the garment. In the van, DANNY and David change into construction worker clothes. They walk to the apartment complex.

"Do you think he is home?" David inquires.

"Not likely. I engaged in casing of the target. He is usually not at home at this time of day," the Israeli agent says.

"How do you think we can enter the apartment complex?" David inquires.

"You will see," the Israeli agent says.

DANNY walks up to the front door of the complex. As they don't possess a key, both patiently wait until someone exits the front door.

A woman approaches the door. "*Terve*," she says. She opens the door, and they both continue to walk up to the apartment.

The two operatives walk to the elevator. The elevator door closes. It rises to the fourth floor, and the doors open. David and DANNY walk out of the elevator and approach the Iranian target's apartment. DANNY knocks on the door. No one responds. He then looks left and right and sees that no one is watching. DANNY proceeds to stick a small pick in the lock. Within seconds, the lock opens. DANNY opens the door.

The Israeli agent and David walk inside. "No problem," the MOSSAD agent says.

They see a small room, which contains a bed, a desk, a computer, and little else.

DANNY boots up the laptop, and he takes a thumb drive and inserts it into the side port. Danny types on the computer and is able to obtain and enter the password. Within minutes, DANNY is searching the laptop's computer files and downloading all information on the laptop. David diligently searches the drawers of the desk and finds a stack of papers. He spots several crudely drawn maps. David takes out his cell phone and snaps several detailed pictures of each piece of paper.

"Let's go. Our target may be getting back home soon," David remarks.

"I'm done," the Israeli agent says.

DANNY and David quickly exit the apartment, continue back to the van, and sit down.

"That was easy . . . almost too easy. Do you trust your informant? How do you know he is an operative?" the MOSSAD agent remarks. He appears to cast doubt on the information about the target being an intelligence operative.

"Of course," David says. He knows DANNY is searching for more information, and he suspects that he may want to steal his source.

"I think a Hezbollah intelligence operative would have taken more precautions," DANNY says. He appears very skeptical, as if to challenge David.

"What did you find in the desk?" the Israeli agent asks.

"I'm not really sure," David says. He remembers that playing dumb is a time-honored rule of intelligence operatives. He will only release the information after the Israelis have released their findings.

"Any idea what information is contained on the target's laptop?" David adds.

"I have to get back with an analysis. It will take time," the Israeli says. "We don't have your huge Langley resources to extract information from computers."

David suspects that DANNY may be lying and delaying to see what the CIA possesses.

"No problem. I will let you know what I find. It's always good to work with the MOSSAD," David says.

"So what do you know about Hezbollah?" the Israeli agent inquires.

David thinks for a moment. "Well, probably less than you. You might want to brief me on what the MOSSAD knows," David says.

"Sorry, I have no time to brief you. I will be in touch. It was nice working with you."

"No problem. It was good to work with you also," David adds. He smiles politely.

David walks back to the United States embassy and enters his office. He downloads his pictures on to his laptop and prints them out. He walks to the printer and proceeds to review the pictures he captured from his apartment. There are various drawings on each with words printed in Farsi. He spots the Finnish word "*Jyväskylä*," which is written next to one of the drawings. There is another drawing that appears to be a house, a picture of the woods, and an address written in Farsi. David transcribes the Farsi into a translator program. The English translation makes it obvious that the numbers are map coordinates. It reads, "*62.2417° N, 25.7417° E.*"

David opens a map program on his laptop and inputs the coordinates into the program. The program quickly zooms into the site and shows details of the area. He is shocked to his core by what he observes. The map turns out to be the exact coordinates of his summer home. David sits back in his seat. He is stunned into silence. *Is the Iranian target associated with the attack on my summer home?* David wonders. He proceeds to draft a cable to Langley headquarters. He writes and sends it:

*From: **Helsinki Station To: CIA Headquarters, limited dissemination**, Joint operation with MOSSAD completed. A number of documents were recovered* *from the apartment during the operation, and an analysis of the target's laptop is being completed. The evidence may have revealed a connection to an assassination attempt on a CIA agent in Jyväskylä. There is no clear connection to the Hezbollah or the threat information provided by IRAN EXILE. I will follow up with IRAN EXILE with additional intelligence. The MOSSAD will engage in a computer analysis. I am happy to follow up with requirements from CIA headquarters to fill any intelligence gaps."*

Chapter 14

A Grim Anniversary

David awakes to the sounds of raindrops striking the outside of the windowpane of his bedroom. With trepidation, he reluctantly rises from bed, showers, and gets dressed. He exits his apartment and proceeds to walk to his apartment's parking lot. David approaches and enters his unlocked car. He sighs for a second, takes out the ignition key from his pocket, and places the key in the ignition. He starts the engine, and the car roars to life. David's car pulls out of his parking spot and enters a small road. He begins the journey from Helsinki to Lohja to view Terhi's grave.

During his journey to southern Finland, David observes the trees lining the side of the road and ponders the good times he experienced with his wife. He remembers spending time fishing on the lake near the summer home, his experience enjoying wood-burning saunas with Terhi, and the quiet silence that permeated his time with her. It's an anniversary that David dreads from the soul of his being. The death of Terhi at the summer home three months ago has changed David. He feels a deep sense of loss and pain. David swore to himself that he would visit his wife's grave during this anniversary, as this is the only time he can take experiencing the emotional pain associated with her death.

David reaches over to the control panel of his car and proceeds to turn on the satellite radio. A Finnish pop tune begins to play in the background. He appears somber, and the feeling of guilt is palpable. *What could I have done differently that day at the summer home to prevent Terhi's death?* David thinks to himself. He stares at the road and the endless rows of trees lining the highway while deep in thought.

After thirty minutes of driving, David is able to see the small south coastal town of Lohja. He spots the city center and the port in the distance. He continues driving to the center of the city and arrives at a small church, which dates from the 12th century and possesses a stone façade. David parks the car and enters the 12th-century structure. David spots an attendant, who is a young woman in her thirties. She is wearing a nametag with the word "Valtonen" written on it, which is attached to her lapel.

"Excuse me, do you speak English?" David asks.

"Yes," the young woman responds.

"I would like to visit the cemetery out back. Is this possible?" David asks.

"I'm sorry. We only provide tours of the church," the woman informs.

"I'm a relative of a person who is buried in the cemetery. Surely, I can view the grave," David says. He seems a little distraught.

"What's the name of your relative?" Valtonen asks.

"Terhi Markoff," David responds.

"I will search our computer records. If I find the grave, I will escort you there. Please wait here," Valtonen informs. She walks in the direction of the back of the church.

David waits inside the small interior of the church. He bides his time viewing the old church icons painted on the walls. These include Jesus's Sermon on the Mount and a rendition of apostles Peter and Mark. David's family has never been very religious. In the Soviet Union, religion was prohibited. He first attended church at his wedding. He remembers Terhi was dressed in a white gown and that all the members of his family were in attendance. It was the happiest time of his life. The young woman reenters the church's interior, breaking David's daydream and jolting him back to reality.

"I am sorry to say that Terhi's body is no longer in the cemetery."

"What do you mean? She was buried here," David questions. He is confused and a little angry. His expression reveals his disbelief.

"Well . . . according to our records, her body was disinterred from her grave and transported to another location," Valtonen says.

"Who would do that? I am her husband. I never agreed to this. Where was Terhi's body transported to exactly? I'm her only relative. Her family was killed in an accident," David remarks. He appears quite distraught.

"Unfortunately, I only possess the name of the company that moved the body. My records indicate that Interex Oy provided the proper paperwork. I can provide other details if you give me your personal information to confirm your relationship."

"Please do. I want to know how this occurred. I never agreed to this," David adds. He takes out his card, which contains his phone number and his contact information at the United States embassy.

"I will be sure to be in touch with you," Valtonen adds.

"Thank you," David says.

David leaves the small church, enters his car, and begins the journey home. As he drives, he makes a phone call to the office on his cell phone. He places the phone on speaker mode and dials.

"Jake, how is it going?" David says.

"Not bad. I read on the web that Minnesota received the first National Hockey League draft pick. The championship may be within our grasp. I'm in a good mood today. How can I assist you?" Jake says.

"I need a big favor. My wife's body was moved from her grave. There is a company called Interex Oy that disinterred her body and moved it to an unknown location. Can you do a name trace on the company?" David asks.

"Yes. What do you want to know about the company?" Jake responds.

"Tell me the company's address and phone number, and do an analysis of who owns it," David says.

"I will get back to you with the information as soon as possible," Jake says.

"Thanks," David says. He proceeds to hang up the phone.

David drives back to Helsinki. He is quiet, emotionally drained, and appears a bit angry. The disappearance of his wife's body has left him shaken to his core.

Chapter 15

Russia on the March

"Prepare for a simulated search-and-destroy mission," a Russian general yells through his military phone. He is located at the Russian Western Military District Headquarters near the Russian–Finnish Karelian border and Russia's Beovets airbase.

Over 10,000 Russian and Belarusian troops march in formation in preparation for war games, which mimic a simulated attack on Finland. Russian M1-8 helicopters can be seen to be flying, along with Mi-24 aircraft, over the skies near the Russian–Finnish border.

Along the Finnish border in Northern Karelia, Finnish troops, comprising two Jaeger companies, observe the Russian troop exercise with interest and alarm. Many soldiers sit at their posts watching and noting the number of Russian troops, types of vehicles used, and military tactics.

A Finnish soldier spots a Russian bomber flying overhead. It enters Finland, violating Finnish airspace. The soldier immediately turns on his radio and communicates with his headquarters. "I just spotted an aircraft flying overhead. It appears to be heading west.

It looks to be a Russian bomber. I'm sure you can spot it on radar," he warns.

Helsinki, Finland

On the radar at the Helsinki command center, the bomber appears to be heading in the direction of the capital. "Scramble our fighters to intercept the aircraft before they reach Helsinki," a Finnish Air Force general orders.

In the Air above Finland

Several Finnish Hornet fighter aircraft, which display Finland's white and blue colors on their sides, take off from an airbase located in eastern Finland with the mission of intercepting the Russian bomber. They quickly approach the Russian bomber, which is escorted by one Russian Bear aircraft fighter.

The Finnish pilot spots the bomber within his sights. He attempts to cut it off from its current trajectory—Helsinki. The Russian fighter quickly responds, jettisoning numerous flares to thwart any possible radar-associated targeting of the bomber.

"We are tracking the aircraft, but cannot stop him without taking hostile actions," a Finnish pilot reports to his commander.

Helsinki, Finland

A Helsinki-based Air Force general picks up the phone at his desk. He looks worried. He calls Finnish Primer Minister Tarja Manninen. "Prime Minister, a Russian bomber is on a trajectory that appears to be a bombing raid on the Finnish capital. What should we do? Shoot it down?"

"Follow it. I will make that decision soon," Tarja remarks. Her expression conveys her deep concern.

In the Air above Finland on the Outskirts of Helsinki

The Russian bomber descends to a lower altitude, flying at 35,000 feet in the air. It opens its bomber doors in preparation for an attack.

The Finnish fighters continue to trail the Russian bomber and fighter, attempting to lock their radar on the bomber in case they receive an order to shoot the bomber out of the sky. The pilot radios Helsinki: "The bomber appears ready for an attack."

Helsinki, Finland

Prime Minister Tarja Manninen sits in her office nervously pondering her options. She picks up the phone and calls President Vladimirovich in Moscow. The phone rings several times. "I would like to speak to the president. I am the Finnish prime minister."

There is a momentary delay. President Vladimirovich enters the line.

"Mr. President, this is the prime minister. Your bomber has violated Finnish airspace and is about to head over Helsinki. Can you call it off? We have friendly relations with you, after all," Tarja Manninen says.

"Tarja, I'm sorry you're alarmed by our aircraft. Where are the Swedes and your European Union friends to help you?" He pauses. "I will call the bomber off. It's only a practice after all. It may not be next time. I would note that we don't bomb with teddy bears either." He hangs up, and the line goes dead.

Tarja hangs up the phone and sits in her office feeling a bit miffed.

In the Air above Helsinki

The Russian bomber's doors slowly close. The plane changes course and maneuvers in an easterly direction, heading back to its base in Karelia.

Chapter 16

Moscow Calling

"When in Moscow, you always feel like something terrible may occur and feel relieved when it doesn't," David's recalls one of his Russian-born relatives recounting to him during his youth in New York City. David ponders this fact while sitting on a flight traveling from Helsinki to the Russian capital. He is planning to see his friend from CIA Headquarters, who is stationed at the United States embassy, and transport a diplomatic pouch from the United States embassy in Helsinki. David understands the unique operational skills required for visiting a hostile environment: plan your trip, be aware of all surveillance, and always have an escape plan. David is traveling to Russia as a United States employee. He hopes he will be able to quietly enter Russia under the radar of Russia's Federal Security Service and other Russian intelligence services.

David walks off the flight upon landing and approaches Russian immigration. He presents his passport to the Russian immigration inspector, who looks suspiciously at David, carefully reviews his passport, and checks her computer system.

"You can go," the inspector says and hands his passport back to him.

David looks through his passport and appears a little confused. He realizes the inspector has not provided his *Belaya Kartushka* (white paper), which all non-Russians are required to possess in order to leave the country. David knows that not possessing a *Belaya Kartushka* could cause him significant problems while visiting the country.

"I need my *Belaya Kartushka*. You did not give it to me with my passport," David demands in Russian.

"So sorry. It was my mistake, Mr. American diplomat. Here you go." The woman smiles slyly, places the white registration paper inside the passport booklet, and hands the passport back to David.

David surmises that Russian immigration did not err and that he must be under the watch of the Russian Federal Security Service, who are seeking to hinder his efforts in Russia. He is wary, as he must carefully consider every move he makes in Russia.

David proceeds to exit the airport. He looks for a cab and is greeted by a driver, who looks to be of Tajikistani origin.

"Where do you want to go?" the driver inquires with a thick accent in Russian.

"The American embassy," David says.

"No problem," the cab driver responds.

David enters the cab, and the car rapidly progresses in an erratic fashion through the usual heavy Moscow traffic. The driver runs through several traffic lights and cuts off other drivers on his way to the United States embassy. David views the trip with worry, as he fears an accident could occur at any moment. He receives a call on his cell phone and answers it.

"David, welcome home," George says and laughs.

"Thanks. I'm not home but have emerged in chaos central. This is better known as the inner ring of Moscow," David retorts.

"Let's meet at a bar next to the embassy. It might be a better venue for our discussion. I will send the address to you in a text," George remarks.

"Sounds good to me. See you soon," David says.

The cab arrives next to the bar at the address that was forwarded to him. David walks out of the cab and proceeds to enter the alcohol establishment. He finds a table and sits down. After a couple of minutes, George, a thirty-something blond-haired man, walks inside the tavern. He is wearing a suit and tie, an overcoat, and a dour expression.

"Sit down, George. It's always nice to see you again," David says. He flashes a friendly smile. He passes the diplomatic pouch to George, who is sitting across the table.

David and George order drinks, and a waitress promptly delivers them to the table.

"Glad to see you're surviving Helsinki. I'm sorry to hear about your wife," George says.

"Thanks. How is the Russian FSB treating you? I hear it can be rough for United States diplomats in Moscow," David asks.

"Well, the Russian FSB enters my apartment four times a week claiming to check the power when they are in fact downloading recording devices placed in strategic areas of my residence. They mess with my laptop when I am not home and also use my bathroom and don't flush the toilet when I am not in my residence," George says. He picks up his club soda and takes a sip.

"Sounds like a relative I know who stayed at my apartment in New York City. I guess the bonus is that if you ever get lost in Moscow, you can ask the FSB agent following you for directions." David chuckles. He picks up his vodka shot and takes one gulp.

Seth Chanowitz

"Do you think we are being watched right now? Russian immigration did not provide me with all the proper documents to stay here. I suspect it was purposeful," David asks.

"I think the FSB probably followed you from your flight into Moscow and will tail you all the way out of the country. Welcome to Russia. Welcome home!" George says and flashes a big grin. His expression turns more serious. "David, you seem different from that last time I saw you. What is going on?" George asks.

David pauses for a moment and takes a sip of his drink. "Terhi's death has changed me. I take everything more serious now. I'm not the same happy individual you knew me as at CIA headquarters two years ago," David divulges.

"I am sorry to hear that. David, I think you should know the arrest of the Russian illegals in the United States has charged up Langley with a new initiative. CIA security is searching for anyone they think could possibly be an illegal or a Russian spy. Your youth in Russian Karelia has now made you a possible suspect. I hear they suspected your wife also," George reveals.

"My wife. That's odd. What do you think might happen?" David asks. He looks very concerned.

"With those CIA counter-intelligence programs, it's hard to know. I would be careful right now. Anything is possible. Don't trust anyone at headquarters. I heard they were suspicious of your wife due to her Finnish nationality," George remarks.

David is quiet for a moment as he ponders the situation. He fidgets with the glass he has placed next to him.

"What do you suggest I should do?" David asks. He appears quite anxious.

"Helsinki may be a good place for you to lay low until things cool off. Trust me on this. A new development will happen, and they will focus their efforts elsewhere. You know how the bureaucrats work in DC," George says. He sighs.

David pauses for a second and appears to be calculating his strategy. "Thanks for the warning. Good to see you again," David says.

"Good seeing you, too. Take care, and be careful. Langley is a minefield. It's best not to trust anyone now," George says.

"Thanks." David shakes George's hand and leaves the bar. He walks over to his hotel, which is located two blocks away. David enters the hotel, heads to the front desk, obtains his room key, and enters his room.

He puts down his luggage for the trip. Immediately, a loud pounding on the front door of his hotel room startles David. He is confused, as he isn't expecting anyone. He slowly approaches the door and looks outside through the door's spy hole. He spots Yuri, who works at the Russian embassy in Helsinki and whom he last encountered at the United States embassy in Helsinki.

"Welcome to Russia," Yuri announces outside his door. He grins.

David is surprised. He opens the door. "Come inside," he says.

Yuri walks in with a bottle of wine in hand. "I heard you were staying in the same hotel, and I decided to see you so that I may provide you with advice about Moscow. It would be rude in Russian culture for me not to assist you." He sits down and smiles.

"It's quite unexpected to see you here. Who told you I was staying here?" David asks.

"That's not important. Listen, David, everything happens for a reason in life. I'm happy to provide you with a list of places to visit. A Russian man like you must need some assistance. I have a friend, Natalia, who will escort you around the city if you are interested," Yuri remarks.

David ponders his next move. "Thanks for the assistance and offer, but I am only here for a day," David says.

"I'm always happy to help you. If you don't have time in Moscow, we can meet again in Helsinki. You have my number. In any case, let's have a glass of fine wine," Yuri adds.

"Perhaps you can assist me. If you know anything out of the ordinary about Interex Oy, let me know. This is for a family-related issue," David asks. David figures a connection might assist in the future, as the truism keeping your friends close and your enemies closer can't hurt.

"I will do some research and get back to you. Well, let us drink to a new friendship," Yuri exclaims. He smiles and holds his glass up in a toast. They both touch glasses and proceed to drink. David sports a friendly smile, though he is wary of this new, dangerous relationship.

Chapter 17

A Russian Source

The chimes of David's cell phone awaken him from a deep sleep at 2:00 a.m. Half-asleep, David frantically attempts to pick up the phone to answer the incoming call. He finds the phone on the table next to his bed and looks at the number calling him, which is displayed on the screen of his smartphone device. He sees that the call might be originating from the embassy and answers it.

"Good morning, David. I'm sorry to wake you up so early," Jake says.

"What happened? Is everything alright?" David states quietly, sounding very groggy.

"Nothing to worry about, but your unique talent is needed immediately. I just wanted to alert you to the arrival of our source, RUSSKAYA PRAVDA, in Finland. You are going to handle him. Your assignment is to meet him at the hotel and extract some good intelligence. I want to know everything that is going on in the inner circle of Russian President Vladimirovich, including the frequency of his bowel movements." Jake chuckles. He adds, "I will send you a copy of all the intelligence information gaps that CIA headquarters wants filled. I have been instructed by CIA HQ that this is a top priority."

"I got it. I'm on my way. Is there anything else I should know?" David asks. David knows this is a great opportunity. RUSSKAYA PRAVDA, which is the source code name for Arkady Steynberg, is a star source for the CIA's Eastern European operations. He is everything you want in a spy. He possesses direct access to obtain actionable intelligence, as he worked with the president as his press secretary and is still part of the president's outer circle. He also founded the Russian government-controlled international media empire, Russia Now, and knows all the major players in the Russian media. Further, he has knowable motivations, as he has fallen from favor in the president's eyes after having used heavy-handed tactics against his rivals and wants revenge. RUSSKAYA PRAVDA also has a good reporting history, as the information he has provided has been found to be accurate. Most importantly, RUSSKAYA PRAVDA's reports have been featured as intelligence in the *Presidential Daily Brief*, which is read by all the power brokers in DC and is viewed as great intelligence by the CIA leadership.

"Meet him at the Hotel Helsinki ASAP. It's a $3,000 a night hotel, so dress for the meeting. He will be waiting for you," Jake says.

David hangs up the phone. He showers, gets dressed, and then proceeds to prepare for his meeting. He logs onto his remote computer and downloads all intelligence gaps that were requested from CIA headquarters, along with the picture of his source.

David conducts an exhaustive security review for surveillance. While looking outside his window, he spots a SUPO car down the street from his residence. He decides that wearing a disguise is needed to avoid detection. He searches around his apartment and finds a bag of disguises. He looks inside and decides to wear a beard, a fake brown-haired wig, and a hat. He looks in the mirror and decides the disguise will work. His preparations for his mission have been completed. David walks out the door of his apartment complex at 3:30 a.m. He quickly sprints for several blocks and spots a cab and hails it. The car slows down and approaches David.

David opens the cab door and enters the cab. "Please take me to the Hotel Helsinki," David says.

"*Joo*," the cab driver responds.

The car proceeds to speed up and transports David through Helsinki.

David arrives at the hotel. He opens the car door and gets out of the cab outside the hotel, which is located close to Helsinki's Harbor. David walks up to the hotel lobby and looks for anyone who could fit the description of his source. He sees a heavyset man with black hair who is wearing a thousand-dollar suit, a designer tie, and a $20,000 diamond-studded Swiss watch. His black hair is slicked back, and he has a day-old beard.

He walks up to him. "How was the weather in Moscow?" David asks.

RUSSKAYA PRAVDA smiles. "The weather is good, but I have heard rumors of bad storms approaching. Let us talk about it in the penthouse suite."

"I will be happy to join you in fifteen minutes," David says. He does not want to appear to be meeting an intelligence operative in public. He walks away and looks for the stairs. He opens the door and walks up nine flights.

David arrives at the ninth floor and walks out of the stairway and into the elevator. He sees a video intercom, which allows him to call up to the penthouse suite. David makes a call up to the penthouse. The phone is answered.

"It's safe to come up," an unidentified man says in thickly accented English and hangs up.

The elevator rises to the top floor. David walks out of the elevator and enters a huge, palatial suite with a 360-degree view of Helsinki. David walks around the suite and sees a gold-lined Jacuzzi; a huge, fully stocked bar filled with alcohol; several giant TV screens; and expensive Finnish Alvar Alto furniture placed throughout the room. He walks into a huge living room and sees two huge, heavily armed bodyguards standing in the corner. He is wearing an earpiece for communication purposes.

"How are you? Welcome to my humble hotel room," RUSSKAYA PRAVDA says. He flashes a friendly smile.

"I'm a little tired but good. How was your flight to Finland?" David asks.

"Not bad. I was not hassled by the SUPO, which sometimes happens when I enter the country. I am on their watch list, it seems. Hope you were able to avoid the surveillance. OK, let's get down to business," RUSSKAYA PRAVDA says and presents a businesslike smile. He motions for his bodyguards to leave the room. They walk out of the room and shut the door.

David sits down in a chair next to RUSSKAYA PRAVDA and takes out his notepad. "I checked, and all is clear. The SUPO was watching me, but I lost them." He pauses. "Do you have any information relating to President Vladimirovich actions against NATO or the Nordic states?"

"No update from our last discussion. The Russian president was meeting with the top military leadership last week. I can't say what his plans are exactly. I heard he has been establishing spy and paramilitary networks in Finland, which he may activate in the event of a war. The teddy bear bombing has angered him immensely. I think the Russian president may engage in some type of action as revenge for the teddy bear bombing. I don't have any information about this, though."

"What do you know about the Russian spy networks?" David questions.

"I need to warn you that Russian intelligence is spearheading a new spying offensive targeting NATO member states and its allies. The Russian president has made intelligence collection a top priority for the government. Even Russia's old Soviet-era "illegal" agents, who were sent to infiltrate Western countries, are being reactivated now. The Russian SVR and FSB have their marching orders and you need to be aware of this." RUSSKAYA PRAVDA pauses and takes out a thumb drive. He adds, "I also heard that Russian intelligence has a good source of information coming from an American located in the Nordic countries. I think the Russian intelligence source is located in Helsinki, Finland, Sweden, or Denmark. I don't have the identity of the American asset. It's a well-guarded secret."

"Do you possess any other information?" David asks.

"I have some position papers from the president's office. This may be of interest. I am working on some great information about the president's shell companies and other illegal assets. I expect good payment. I will be in contact soon." The Russian source passes the thumb drive to David.

"We will deposit the money in your usual account. Please sign this paper," David says. He places a piece of paper on the table.

RUSSKAYA PRAVDA signs the paper and gives it back to David. "Good. I'm about to buy another flat in London and am looking for another one in New York City. This will assist," the Russian source says.

David walks out of the penthouse apartment. He takes the elevator down to the hotel's lobby and then walks to the tram and proceeds to travel back to Kallio and his apartment. Upon entry into his apartment, David places all of his things on the bed and takes a nap.

At 8:00 a.m. the same morning, David awakes. He checks his email and quickly opens a message from

Jake marked urgent: *I think you need to read this. Hope you are well. Give me an update as soon as possible. Jake.* David sees there is a link within the email. He proceeds to open the link. It reads, *Arkady Steynberg, former Russian Presidential Press Secretary and founder of the Russian International TV service, Russia Now, was found dead in his hotel room this morning. He is rumored to have died of a heart attack. The Finnish police have arrived at the scene and are conducting an autopsy.*

A chill goes down David's spine. He is deeply worried. He wonders, *Was I followed by Russian intelligence or the SUPO? Was Arkady killed by Russian intelligence?*

Chapter 18

A Meeting with the Ambassador

It's July 2014, and David is conducting an interview with a United States citizen in distress who is visiting Finland on holiday.

"Welcome to the United States embassy. So tell me, how I can assist you?" David questions while sitting in the interviewing room, which is situated in the Consular section.

"I lost my passport and my purse, which contained all my money." A twenty-year-old woman from Seattle, Washington sits in a chair on the opposite side of the table. Her expression reveals that she is clearly distressed.

"How did this happen?" David asks. He writes on his notepad.

"I was attending a heavy metal rock festival in Oulu. I got drunk, slept with a guy, and the next morning, I woke up to discover that all my things were gone," Samantha says.

"What is your name?" David asks.

"Samantha Smith. I'm from Seattle, Washington. I am surprised I was robbed here. My grandparents are from Finland and I heard from them that the country is very safe," she responds.

"Did you report this crime to the police?" David asks. He writes on his notepad.

"No. I don't speak Finnish and don't know the number for the police in Finland either. I was in the middle of the Finnish countryside and did not know who to turn to for assistance," Samantha says.

"I think we can help you with some funds to allow you to get back to the United States if that is required," David responds.

The phone at David's desk rings.

"Samantha, excuse me for a moment while I take this phone call." David picks up the phone. "This is Jake. Can you walk up to the office now?"

"I am currently interviewing a United States citizen, but I will be there momentarily." David hangs up the phone.

"I will give you several forms you can fill out. A woman in our program office will be able to assist you if you need money to return to the United States," David says.

"Thank you," Samantha says.

David gets up from his seat and walks up to the security officer's office. He puts his identification card in the door's ID slot, and the door opens. He walks into the office.

"Good afternoon," David remarks to several employees whom he sees upon entry. He approaches another door, which is marked "Authorized Individuals Only." He places his identification card in a slot next to the door. The door then clicks open. David sees that Jake is sitting at the desk, and lying before him are several documents with the words "Top Secret" written on them.

"Good to see you, David." Jake flashes a friendly smile.

"How are you? What's the latest from Washington DC?" David questions.

"I'm good. Our Washington headquarters is getting all spun up about the Russians now. Intelligence reports indicate that Russian troops are concentrating on the border of Finland," Jake informs. He adds, "I have left the latest intelligence on your desk, which is all sources of information to include *SIGINT*, *OSINT*, and *HUMIT*. You can check all the information that is in our system if you would like. David, I'm sure you are aware that intelligence analysts at HQ put way too many caveats in their intelligence assessments, so it's hard to extract definite information from anything you read. Consequently, I will give you interpretation of the intelligence from the region, which indicates a growing Russian hostility toward the United States and the NATO alliance."

"Thanks for the brief. I can tell you that I have written way too many cables of great analysis that most people only have time to read the first paragraph of at HQ. It's crazy . . . Jake. I'm wondering. Is there any news on the trace of the company Interex Oy, which moved my wife's remains?" David asks. He appears quite interested in the information.

"The research I did revealed that the name of the registered business you provided is in fact a shell company of a Russian-based firm, which is located in St. Petersburg, Russia. That is all I know, unfortunately. Those shell companies are not easy to track. I read your report about your meeting with RUSSKAYA PRAVDA. I know the Finnish police are investigating his death. How was your meeting with our source, AMERICANO?" Jake questions. He's sitting at his desk typing on his computer.

"I wrote up a cable for CIA headquarters describing what happened. I hope you read it. I wanted it forwarded with the monthly CIA station report," David asks. He approaches Jake's desk.

"I read a little of it. Unfortunately, I have been busy with the ambassador and had to follow up on several tasks from the CIA's Langley headquarters. You had the bad luck to be in a biker gang-connected shootout in Finland. That is quite unusual here. There are lots of guns in this country, but robbery or gun-related crime is rare," Jake says. He looks up from his computer for a moment.

"I'm lucky to be alive. I have to say that I never imagined a large motorcycle gang scene in Helsinki, but I have heard about the biker wars in Denmark and Sweden of the 1990s. That was when many United States-originating criminal biker gangs formed in the Nordic countries, and rival gangs fought each other in turf battles using explosive devices," David says.

"I'm waiting on some actionable intelligence from our source related to foreign individuals entering Finland for a possible assassination," David says. He seems a little excited.

"The intelligence your source obtained about the Somali–Finnish jihadist was good," Jake adds. He looks up from his computer.

"I would like to task our source to obtain more details about that hit," David remarks.

"David, we have several other tasks assigned to us from Langley, and I don't think that is priority. The last threat from the Iranian did not turn out to be a Hezbollah agent. I would drop it. You get a great deal of background noise with false information about possible threats currently, as the terrorist threat level is relatively high worldwide," Jake remarks.

"Yes sir," David remarks. David feels quite upset but follows orders.

Jake continues typing on his computer for several minutes. "David, there is an event that might be of interest to you. I have several tickets for an ice hockey game. Would you like to go?" Jake asks. He looks up at David from his computer.

"Ice hockey during the summer?" David questions. He appears a little confused.

"This is Finland. They are ice hockey crazy here. Even when they win the under-eighteen World Ice Hockey Championship, the whole country celebrates," Jake says. He smiles.

"When is the game?" David asks. He looks a little excited.

"Tonight at 7:00 p.m. The United States ambassador to Finland will be there also. It will also provide the added benefit of face time with the ambassador," Jake says.

"Thanks for the invite. Sounds good. I will show up there tonight," David says.

"You buy the beer to return the favor," Jake quips. He flashes a big grin.

David walks out of the office and returns to his desk, which is located in the Consular Affairs section. He looks at several emails that have entered his inbox on his computer.

One encrypted email has been sent from his friend at CIA headquarters. David uses the computer software to unencrypt it. He read it: *Greetings, hope all is well with you in Helsinki. The pressure is being upped here. Beware! You might be purged by CIA security.*

At 5:00 p.m., David leaves his office at the United States embassy and boards a tram back to Kallio. He sits down upfront on the tram, as all the seats have been taken. As he looks out the window, David observes that the clouds in the sky are turning gray and threatening. The possibility of rain appears likely. David searches for his umbrella in his bag and briefcase but can't find it. He curses to himself. He is startled, as an unknown individual taps him on his back. He immediately turns around and sees SUPO Agent Pia Hjelt.

"You can borrow my umbrella." Pia smiles. She hands David an umbrella.

"Why, thank you, Pia. Does it contain an implanted SUPO listening device, too?" David takes the small umbrella from Pia's hand. He smiles and laughs a little. "So, how is your running progressing?" David inquires.

"Good. I'm now training for the Helsinki City Marathon. I am hoping to complete the marathon in under three hours," Pia retorts. "So can we talk for a moment?" Pia asks.

"How can I resist a discussion with a beautiful Finn?" David smiles slyly.

David and Pia walk off the tram at the Kallio stop and head to the Helio Café, which is located on the main boulevard near central Bear Park.

The café has an arts and crafts décor. There are seven tables, and hanging wind mobiles are present throughout the café. David sits down with Pia at a small table located in the back of the café.

"David, so what were you doing hanging out at the Metal Barri?" Pia questions. She looks quite serious.

"Finns never have any time for small talk? You could buy me a coffee if you are engaging in an interrogation. Isn't that normal police practice in Finland?" David remarks.

"Seriously, I'm beginning to wonder about you," Pia says. She spouts a serious expression.

"I provided the SUPO with all I know related to my contact with Bergstrom," David says. David attempts to appear as innocent as possible. He pauses for a second. He decides the best way to deal with the accusation. David assesses that he must have been followed to the bar by a SUPO surveillance team. "Listen, Pia, I was at Metal Barri, as it's an undiscovered area of Helsinki. I like visiting unexplored areas of Helsinki. Since I know you are interested in all my activities in Helsinki, I think you should volunteer to take me to a better place on a date? The report will be more interesting at least," David adds. He flashes a big grin.

"Not so fast, Mr. Markoff. The SUPO has some issues with you." Pia points her finger.

"I think the SUPO is seeing a connection with the CIA to every American living in Helsinki. I'm unhappy to report I am just a boring consular official. I will ask my supervisor if there are any top-secret missions she can send me on if that will make me seem more interesting to your intelligence organization." David chuckles.

Pia sits in her chair, silent for a moment. "OK, David. Should you know anything of interest to the SUPO, please contact me. Your cooperation will keep you in good standing with our organization. We don't have to expel you from Finland for working for the CIA. Let's work out some cooperation. Keep me updated on the latest activity associated with biker gangs, and I will overlook your meeting at the Metal Barri for now." Pia appears a little perturbed.

"You can be very demanding. Should I discover something, I will be more than happy to alert you." David looks at his watch. "I don't mean to cut our conversation short, but I have to head to the Finland v. USA ice hockey match. It's always nice seeing you, though," David says.

"Talk to you later. Remember what I said," Pia warns.

David gets up from his chair and then looks for a cab and hails it. He enters the cab and is driven to the Helsinki International Ice Hockey Arena. He exits the cab and walks up to the arena's entrance.

"*Terve*. I am David Markoff. I am scheduled to go to a party located in the skybox. My name is on a list to attend the party," David states.

"*Joo,*" a Finnish woman remarks. The woman then types David's first and last names into her computer. "Welcome, Mr. Markoff. You can walk to the elevator and go to the sixth floor, where the skybox is located."

"Thanks." David smiles.

David walks down a hall and onto the elevator. He presses the button for the sixth floor.

The elevator ascends, and it opens. David walks out of the elevator and enters a huge party room. The room contains a bar stocked with alcohol. He can see that beautiful women are mingling in abundance freely through the area, a DJ is playing Swedish and American electronic music, and a great view of the ice hockey rink surface below can be viewed. David peers out the window and sees from below that the arena is filled to capacity. The ice has the United States and Finnish flags printed on it.

David walks around the party room and spots Jake sitting with a beer in hand.

"David, I am glad you were able to attend the game. I think you met Ambassador Cliff Armstrong before," Jake remarks.

"Yes, I saw you when I first arrived," David says.

"So how are you adjusting to life in Finland?" Cliff questions. He takes a sip of his beer.

"It seems nice. It's several thousand miles from Washington DC, which is a big positive on my end." David chuckles.

"Come sit down with me, as the game is starting," Cliff states. He leads the way to several seats situated close to the window of the skybox.

Dave sits down. The game progresses with the Finns scoring a goal in the first period.

"I hear you're an attorney," Ambassador Cliff Armstrong remarks while holding a Finnish beer in his hand.

"I am. I have to be honest. I practiced law for a very short period of time," David responds.

"No matter to me. I have a few good attorneys at my hedge fund company in New Jersey," Cliff says. He takes another sip of his beer.

"So, what do you see as your goals for your time in Finland?" David asks.

"Nice you ask. Actually, the president sent me here to promote American business. The economic situation is not good in the United States after the debt crisis. We have to work hard to have United States companies succeed internationally. Finland is important. David, are you a true American?" Cliff looks serious.

"Sure, my family came from the USSR and immigrated to the United States. We may be immigrants, but we like the United States and are proud to be citizens here," David says.

"I'm sure I'm going to like you then. We need people here to promote America to the Finns. The Russians are gaining in economic power with all the oil and natural gas they are exporting. We need to outflank them," Cliff retorts. He seems animated as he talks.

"I'm more than happy to assist you in any way I can in the future," David remarks.

"That's what I like to hear. You're a team player! I have other people to talk to, but we have to get together in the future," Cliff remarks.

"Sound good to me. Thanks," David says.

The ambassador gets up from his chair and walks away. David sits in his seat and watches the rest of the game. The Finns end up beating the United States by a score of 3 to 1.

After the game, David leaves the stadium and returns to his apartment building. When he arrives at the front of his apartment complex, he grabs his keys from his backpack.

He is startled by the sound of a voice and a hand, which touches his backside. David responds by drawing his gun.

"Relax, *mi amigo*," Lopez says. He walks out of the shadows and toward David.

"How did you find out where I live?" David questions. He looks quite angry and paranoid. He puts his gun back in its hiding place under his belt.

"I know someone who owns this apartment complex," Lopez says. He smiles slyly.

"We have to meet in secure locations or engage in a *dead drop* for an information exchange, as the SUPO is watching," David warns. His expression reveals he is quite angry.

"Don't be fucking ungrateful. I checked. The Finnish police were not following me. I have obtained great intelligence for you. I got the information about the hit you wanted. Here are the details. You can thank me later with lots of cash," Lopez says. He curses in Spanish.

Lopez hands the envelope to David and walks back into the shadows. David walks up to his apartment and opens the door. David walks to the window and looks outside for any sign of surveillance being conducted. He sees none and sits down at his desk. David proceeds to open the envelope and reads it. The note states, *There is a scheduled hit on a woman named Katya Neimi, who lives in Helsinki at 14 Hietalahtiranta Katu. The assassination should occur within the next several months. The person or organization that has scheduled the hit cannot be identified.* David is stunned.

Bergstrom is killed and now someone wants to kill another person associated with Outlandish PR. David wonders what his next move should be. He thinks, *Should I alert the SUPO, tell the CIA, or keep the information secret?*

Chapter 19

The Washington DC Visit

His heart is racing, he is rapidly inhaling and exhaling, sweat slowly drips from his forehead, and the sounds of gunshots ring in his ears. In a second, David awakes with a gasp. David's eyes open, and he calms down as he realizes that he is safe within his bed. The light of Finland's midnight sun glares on his bed from his bedroom window within his apartment in Kallio. "Another nightmare," David mutters to himself. His dreams of that terrible morning at the summer home seem to repeat nightly as if being haunted by the absence of Terhi within his life is not enough. He feels quite dour.

David is startled by the loud tone blaring from his smartphone, which reveals an incoming call. He reaches over to his night table, grabs the phone, and looks at the number. He recognizes it as Jake and answers the call.

"Good morning, Jake. This must be an emergency. I usually don't see or hear from you until after your morning visit to the Foggy Bottom Café at the United States embassy," David says.

"No emergency. It's not like Minnesota lost the cup championship finals or anything on that scale. I need to alert you to the fact that you are wanted in Washington DC. Pack your stuff, get your passports, and head to Helsinki Vantaa International airport to catch a flight to Dulles International Airport in Washington DC as soon as possible. Bring suits. I know you analyst types at the CIA sometimes dress very casual. This is a suit-and-tie meeting."

"Jake, I think you should remember that I'm a trained CIA operative. I have a suit and tie. It's those analysts at Langley who dress like they are homeless," David quips. He thinks it's very ironic that he is identified as an analyst. David always identified with the operations types who risk their lives attempting to obtain actionable intelligence from sources.

"A suit and tie sounds good to me," Jake says.

"Do you have any idea of the subject of the meeting?" David questions. David appears concerned and apprehensive.

"Too highly classified for me, evidently. I have no idea," Jake says.

"This sounds strange. I wonder what's up in Langley," David remarks. David's survival instincts make him suspect that Jake is withholding information.

Something seems not quite right, though he has no information to support his fears.

"Sorry about my lack of intelligence. Give my regards to the Washington DC headquarters folks. Hope you can avoid anything related to computer slide presentations. Those presentations can be deadly boring at the Washington DC headquarters. I have called the embassy motor pool. A driver will pick you up and drive you to the airport," Jake says.

"Will do," David quips. David's concern grows, as he has heard there are many purges going on there. Could he be next? Is this the reason for the meeting? David's mind fills with possible explanations.

David puts the phone down, packs his things, and begins to walk out of his apartment. His cell rings again, and he recognizes the number as Jake's.

"Hey, you are needed outside your apartment now. Have a good trip," Jake says.

"Thanks!" David remarks.

David walks outside wearing a suit and tie with his suitcase in hand. He opens the front door of his apartment complex and is startled to see United States ambassador to Finland, Cliff Armstrong, standing outside his car. He is sporting his trademark large grin.

"Get in. We both have to go to Helsinki-Vanta International Airport, and I need to practice my Russian." Cliff laughs and waves for David to approach the car.

"Thanks for the ride." David grins. He appears surprised beyond belief.

The ambassador's driver takes David's luggage and places it in the trunk. Both the ambassador and David get in the sedan, and they begin traveling to the airport.

"How are you liking Finland?" Cliff inquires. He looks at his incoming messages on his phone as he travels.

"I like the Finnish nature. The amount of small talk can be rare in Helsinki, though," David says.

"David, Finns are not known for small talk. They only tend to talk to you too much when they are drunk." He pauses. "I am heading for a NATO defense conference. I know you are only a consular employee, but your Russian knowledge is helpful for the trip. I like the fact that you were a good athlete from what I hear," Cliff says.

"I am more than happy to provide you with my opinion and suggestions about running a triathlon if you want." David sprouts a big grin.

"So, what do you think of President Vladimirovich? Can he be trusted?" Cliff questions. He looks at his email for a moment but continues to listen to David.

"Russia is in a nationalist mode now. I would say that depends on what his interests are presently," David says.

"What do you think of the Finnish military? Are they an effective force?" Cliff asks.

"Finland's military is small but has a can-do attitude that has the potential to hinder the best of militaries. Russia's military may be too big for them. The whole Finnish military could fit inside a United States military base in Texas," David says.

"I think you should join a group I am a member of some time. It meets at a small Russian-themed bar close to the United States embassy. We all speak Russian, talk about Russian literature, and drink vodka," Cliff states in Russian.

"I would be happy to join you. I can't resist a swig of Russian vodka also," David responds.

"Welcome to Helsinki-Vanta International Airport," the embassy driver announces.

"Where are you staying in Washington DC?" the ambassador inquires.

"The email I received says my hotel is located in the Georgetown Waterfront. It's the Potomac Residences," David reports.

"Sounds like you have a good hotel. It was good talking to you. We will be in touch when you get back." Cliff smiles and puts his hand out for David to shake.

David shakes his hand. "Thanks. You have a good trip also."

David walks into the airport, spots the airport's new sauna, the modernist décor, and the clean and new-looking interior. He then boards a flight from Helsinki to Dulles International Airport. He is deep in thought. The reason for this trip is a mystery. He speculates that the CIA misses him at Langley, which could be the reason for his sudden recall. In the CIA, nothing is ever what it seems, and making sense of anything is like reading palms.

After an eight-hour flight, David lands at Washington-Dulles International Airport. He grabs his luggage and then looks around. He spots a man wearing a suit and tie. He also carries a sign stating "Markoff."

He walks up to the man and shows his agency credentials. "I am Markoff."

"Very well. Let's head to the car." The man looks quite dour, is wearing a blue suit and tie, and seems emotionless.

David walks to the awaiting car and gets in the backseat. The man enters the front seat and starts to drive. They both head to Langley, VA. There is silence in the car as they travel for fifteen minutes. They arrive at the gate of the CIA complex.

"Make sure you remember to return your temporary badge when you leave," the driver mutters.

The car stops at the gate, a guard checks David's ID, and the gate opens, which allows the vehicle to enter the facility. The gleaming edifice of the CIA headquarters emerges into view as David's car approaches the parking lot. David sees the sprawling complex of buildings, which consist of a modernist glass design that is atypical for the design of the United States government buildings. As David catches his first glimpse of the CIA complex in the backseat of the car, a feeling of paranoia grows within him. He knows the CIA trusts no one, and everyone may be considered a suspect. He is worried about the visit, as the reason for his meeting is unclear. David wonders, *Will I be purged?*

"You're here," the driver announces. "I will be ready to pick you up when you have to travel to your hotel," he adds.

"Thanks for the lift," David remarks. He hands the driver a tip.

David exits the car, walks into the building, and shows his government ID. The guard takes his card reader out and runs David's ID within the computer system.

"You will have to wait for a minute," the man announces. "You will need an escort in this building," he adds.

A young, clean-cut man in his thirties with brown hair walks out wearing a blue suit and black tie. "You're David Markoff?" he questions.

"Yes, that's me," David says. He sports a friendly but professional smile.

"Walk with me. I'm John Schultz. We are headed to the basement of the new office building," he says. John points the way.

Both walk down the CIA corridors along the white marble floors. The hallways at the agency contain beautiful paintings hung on the walls. The CIA seal is prominently placed on the floor throughout the building. David walks down a staircase with John and enters an area marked "CIA Operations Section." They both walk through a maze of nondescript white cubes and offices. David enters a small room, which contains pictures of the DC skyline, which includes the Washington Monument and the Capitol building, hung on the walls.

"Sit down." John flashes a friendly smile. He nonverbally points to an unoccupied seat.

"Sure," David responds. David feels quite tense.

"I want to let you know that we have an important mission for you, but first, we need you to assist us. We have problems with people leaking information outside our organization. Please walk into the other room, and we will have you undergo a polygraph," John says.

David is unnerved. No one trusts anyone in this organization. They only suspect everyone could be leaking classified information, breaking the rules in someway, or could be involved in activity for a foreign intelligence organization. David feels a little nervous, as he did not report Pia's sexual advance or his meeting with Russian intelligence. He walks into the adjacent office. The polygraph records responses to questions and analyzes whether the person is telling the truth. He spots a man sitting next to a polygraph machine, and a chair is placed next to it.

The heavyset man straps an armband onto David's right arm. The armband is attached to a recording instrument. "I'm going to ask you several questions. Just relax," the man quietly instructs.

"That's easy for you to say," David observes. David sports a sullen expression.

"OK, have you ever worked for any intelligence other the CIA?" the man asks.

"No, I have not," David responds to the question. He slowly breathes in and out and tries to keep calm. This is the key to passing a polygraph. The polygraph's pen records a line onto a paper connected to the device as it tracks David's reactions to each question.

"Do you possess loyalty to any country other than the United States?" the man asks.

"No," David remarks forcefully. Again, the polygraph recorder does not react.

"Are you telling the truth?" the man asks slowly.

"Yes," David remarks. Again, there is no response on the paper.

"Are you hiding anything from the CIA?" the man inquires.

"No." David relaxes. He slowly breathes in and out. The paper again records David's reaction.

"Did you kill your wife?" the man asks.

David is a little shocked and angered by the question. He tries to calm himself down and answers slowly. "No. Of course not!"

The man sitting next to him orders, "We are done now. You can go to the other room and wait for Mr. Schroeder."

David takes off his armband to monitor his pulse. He gets up from his seat and walks to a chair in the next room. He sits alone for several minutes. He is nervous and feels a little shell-shocked.

John Schroeder walks into the room. "Please come with me."

David gets up from his chair and walks through a series of cubes. He enters an area marked "restricted." He opens a door, and sitting there, he sees two men wearing suits and ties. David walks to the table, pulls out the chair, and sits down.

"Before I tell you about the polygraph, I want you to know we are here to brief you on an important operation. We know you have been exiled to Helsinki, and this is a good way to get back into the mix here," John Schroeder briefs.

"I'm listening," David says. He sits up in his chair and wonders what John's true motivations are for providing him with the information.

"We have received a contact from a Belarus-based KGB operative who is traveling to Helsinki. His name is Ivan Mikhailovich, and he will be known from now on as MINSK EYES. He needs to be handled in the correct way. He has contacted us. Our analysts have done a workup on him and believe that he may be a good source and could potentially sway a new Belarus government. He is closely associated with a KGB operative, Valerie Igorovich, who is a powerbroker in the Lukashenko government. You need to assist him in Helsinki to obtain as much intelligence about Russian and Belarus operations. We have reason to believe that he may be involved in organizing a coup attempt against the pro-Russian government," John briefs. He hands a copy of an assessment to David.

David looks at the brief. It states:

SENIOR INTELLIGENCE BRIEF

Directorate of Intelligence, Europe Branch

Belarus Government Coup Possible Due to Russian President Vladimirovich's Pressure to Incorporate It into Russia

- **A variety of intelligence sources indicate that the Belarus dictatorship is increasingly split into a pro-Belarus independence and Pro-Russian incorporation faction. A government split may lead to a possible government coup against the dictatorship or a possible crackdown and purging of the government of anti-Russian elements before declaring Belarus as part of the Russian state.**

- **KGB head, Valerie Igorovich, who leads the Belarus government pro-independence faction, may seek power due to the dictatorship's unpopularity resulting from the economic downturn and the government's mismanagement of the economy.**

We possess no specific information relating to the date a military coup may occur.

David looks up from the briefer. "I think the SUPO may be tailing me. Is Mikhailovich engaging in activity that may possibly jeopardize Finland's security?" David asks.

"Don't worry about that. You know all the counter-surveillance techniques to thwart the SUPO.

This is coming from the fifth floor. In other words, this is a high-priority project with White House awareness," John says.

"Yes, sir," David retorts.

"There may be a person leaking information to the Russians in our offices in the region. We brought you here to DC as you speak Russian fluently, and we need to keep this operation as compartmentalized as possible. Don't discuss this information with Jake," John says.

"I understand. I will keep my mouth shut as usual," David responds.

"I just wanted to let you know that was not a real polygraph you underwent. We trust you, but wanted to gauge your reaction," John says.

"I guess . . . thanks for the confidence," David says. He rolls his eyes.

David gets up from the meeting a little rattled. He is very jet-lagged and longs for a bed to sleep in. He walks out of the CIA headquarters building. He spots his car and motions for the driver to pick him up and transport him to his hotel. David enters the car and travels to Washington DC. After twenty minutes in the car, he enters Georgetown, which is teeming with tourists and has an old colonial feel to it. He sees the

Potomac River, which flows along the city's border, and the Key Bridge, which connects Washington DC to the state of Virginia, can also be viewed in the distance.

"Wait for the word if anything is needed. If not, then you will leave on another flight to Helsinki," the driver says.

"Thanks," David mentions.

David's cell phone rings. He takes the phone out of his pocket and places it next to his ear.

"Hello, this is Sasha."

"Hey, I have not heard from you in ages. How is the family in Minneapolis?" David says.

"Well, the family here is doing nicely. We need a favor from you, as we are having a problem with one of my cousins. We heard you are working at the Department of State in Helsinki, and I obtained your number from a search of your name on the Internet," Sasha says.

"Sasha, tell me. What problem are you experiencing?" David asks.

"Jaanika Olson. Your cousin is trapped in Belarus, and no one can help. We need someone to help her get out of prison," Sasha remarks.

"I will see what I can do. Please send me Jaanika's personal email, and I will try to do the best that I can," David remarks.

"OK. Give me a call if you have any information. This is causing our family to worry greatly. Finland is a really safe place, and we never thought that something would happen to her," Sasha remarks. Her voice reveals she is quite unnerved.

"I promise, I will try to help you. Please say hello to all. Goodbye," David adds.

David looks at his email. He sees Jaanika's email address and sends a message to her. He begins to type: *I am in Helsinki and work at the United States embassy. If you need any help, please email me. I will do what I can to get you out of Belarus. Your cousin, David Markoff.*

"This is your hotel," the driver announces.

"Thanks for your assistance," David says.

David takes his suitcase out of the car and brings it inside the hotel. He proceeds to the hotel's front desk and obtains a door key.

David walks into his hotel room, shuts his hotel room door, puts down his clothes, and immediately goes to sleep.

David is abruptly awakened by the sounds of two men at his front door attempting to break into his hotel room. He hears two gunshots directed at the keyhole of his hotel door. David jumps out of bed. He is terrified and flees to the bathroom. He locks the bathroom door and opens the bathroom window.

Two armed, black-clad men break open David's front door and appear to be searching for David.

David can hear the two men outside the bathroom door. There are several loud sounds coming from the front of the bathroom door. He looks out the window and sees it's only one story down to the ground. He is alarmed by the sound of the men attempting to open the bathroom door, and he decides to jump out the window. With one swift leap, he jumps and lands on his feet on the pavement. He runs in the direction of the front of the hotel and heads to the front desk. He sees a woman and warns, "Someone has attempted to kill me. Call the police."

"Wait in the security office. We will have a security officer guard you until they get here," the hotel employee directs.

David walks to the hotel's security office. He is breathing heavily and sweating.

"Are you OK?" a hotel guard inquires.

"Yes, I'm a little shell-shocked and jet-lagged," David responds.

David has another flashback from that terrible day at his summer cottage in Finland; it is replaying in his mind. He wonders, *Who is trying to kill me?*

Chapter 20

A Belarus Source

In a cramped room containing maps, computers, and a computer display within an unidentified location near Minsk, several men dressed in military uniforms sit in their chairs within small, drab cubicles. The men are watching their computer screens intently or answering the phones located at their desks.

One man, who is wearing a military uniform that identifies his membership in the Belarus military intelligence, sits in a chair along with other military officers. He is intently drafting a report for the military command. He is in his mid-twenties, possesses light blond hair, and has brown eyes.

A man in his mid-fifties walks into the room. He is wearing a uniform with lapels that signify his rank of general within the Belarus armed services.

He walks up to the young soldier. "Vitaly, what is the latest intelligence associated with American and NATO flight patterns the last few days? I need this information as soon as possible," the military officer orders.

"Yes, sir." Vitaly rises quickly from his chair and salutes the general.

Vitaly sits down and intently begins typing at his desk. He drafts a report. His cell phone is lying on his desk. He receives a text. Vitaly reaches for the phone and reads the message: *You want to join me at a Bansky bar tonight?* He knows this is the code for a meeting.

At 5:00 p.m., Vitaly completes his intelligence report. He files it. He exits his desk, walks through two controlled doors, and then walks out of the secret military facility. He enters his car and drives it through the streets of Minsk. After his arrival in central Minsk, Vitaly parks his car. He seems a little nervous and looks around for any signs of danger. Vitaly walks to a small café, which is located near downtown, and sits down. He orders coffee and waits impatiently. After a few minutes, another man approaches him and sits down at the table.

"Good to see you, Mikhail. We don't hang out much anymore. You have changed from your days as a member of our Belarus punk band," Vitaly remarks. He looks a little more relaxed.

"How is the military world going for you?" Mikhail questions. He plays with his cell phone, which is lying on the table, for a moment.

"I think our generals want to start World War III in Europe at the moment. My father was an intelligence officer, and I'm following the family tradition," Vitaly adds. His expression reveals his unhappiness. "I hear your opposition blog, New Belarus, is very popular now. Almost everyone I know reads it," he adds, changing the subject.

"Yeah, it's read by over half a million visitors now, not including the KGB. I have a team of people who also engage in live streaming and video. We mostly focus on keeping people aware of Russian propaganda, and we also post articles criticizing the government. After my posts, I usually receive a visit from the KGB threatening me, my wife, family members, and my future prospects," Mikhail says.

Vitaly momentarily sits back in his chair. "Listen, Mikhail, I have some important information for you. I will forward it to you at the appropriate time. I know that Russian president Vladimirovich is not happy with the Finns and Estonians. I am also aware you are working with many people in opposition to Lukashenko. I am hoping that you may know people connected to Estonia and Finland. Get the information to them. They will be able to use it for maximum benefit," Vitaly adds.

"Can you tell me what the information is exactly?" Mikhail asks.

"All that I can tell you is that it will be useful and important to their countries," Vitaly says.

"I loved the Finns, who conducted the teddy bear drop. It gave me hope for a future for Belarus," Vitaly says.

"Hope is what we are about in the opposition. We demonstrate against the rigged elections by the dictatorship, despite being jailed, beaten, and tortured by the KGB. Belarusians deserve more that just surviving day to day or being forced to leave the country. I continue the struggle, despite the challenges, for the sake of a better future," Mikhail says. He smiles and pounds his fist on the table in jubilation.

"Wait for the appropriate time, and I will get the information to you. This is a very delicate operation. I am being watched closely," Vitaly adds. He drinks a sip of his coffee.

"I will do anything you want and trust you. We are old friends, after all. I know people who are Estonian who can assist us," Mikhail remarks. He looks at his cell phone momentarily.

Vitaly lifts his glass. "We need to drink to something special," he remarks and flashes a friendly smile.

"How about we drink to hope for Belarus and, of course, to our old punk band," Mikhail remarks. He lifts his glass, and they both strike each other's glass in a toast, which results in a clinking sound.

"That's it. I like the sound of that," Vitaly says.

"I will be in contact with you soon about the information," Vitaly remarks. He cracks a little smile. He gets up from the table and walks away.

Chapter 21

Jaanika's Revenge

Jaanika Olson sits in her dark cell on a moldy mattress. She hums a beautiful Estonian melody to entertain herself. Her face appears quite thin, and her eyes are red and bloodshot. On her arms and back are the distinct marks that are evidence of the torture she has suffered at the hands of her interrogator. A woman, who is Slavic in appearance, possesses black hair, and wears a gray uniform, walks up to Jaanika's cell and opens it. "You come," she demands.

"Where is my lawyer? I want to talk with the United States embassy," Jaanika demands. She feels irate at the fact that the KGB would hold her without charging her with an offense.

"You come. You will go to judge," the surly woman orders Jaanika. She points in the direction in which Jaanika is to walk.

Jaanika slowly and reluctantly rises from her bed and stands upright in her cell.

"Your hands," the woman orders Jaanika.

Jaanika reluctantly complies. She puts her hands out. The woman guard opens the cell door and then places handcuffs on Jaanika.

"This way," the woman guard orders in Russian.

Jaanika slowly walks out of her cell and follows the guard down a long, dimly lit white hallway that seems to go on endlessly. As she walks, she hears the echoes of the moans and screams of other prison inmates, who are possibly being beaten and tortured within their cells.

The guard opens the door to exit the interior of the detention center. As the door opens, the light of the sun stuns Jaanika for moment. She pauses to enjoy the sight.

"Come," the huge guard orders impatiently.

Jaanika walks into the prison courtyard and past the guard's station. She sees a man in uniform; he motions for her to walk into a black, Russian-made van. The guard opens the van's back door.

"In here," the guard orders in Russia. He guides her with his hand.

Jaanika enters the van and proceeds to sit down on a small bench. The door is closed behind her.

Jaanika feels tired and sleepy. She rests on the small bench inside the van. The van starts to gain speed, and the roar of the engine can be heard inside the van. The bumps of the road are felt in the van as it travels through the Belarus countryside. Jaanika is jostled in her seat and struggles to maintain her balance.

After thirty minutes, a loud, hideous bang can be heard originating from outside the van. Jaanika is frightened to her core. She is terrified as she is flung against the van's walls by the momentum as the vehicle swerves violently left and right. The van flies off the road. It lands on the ground with a loud thud and slides for several seconds, which causes a screeching sound, which seems to Jaanika to last forever. Her head violently strikes the side of the van, and she falls out of consciousness.

Jaanika wakes up and seems disoriented. She is alarmed by the smell of gasoline and the scent of a smoldering fire. She stands upright in the van, despite feeling awful and having a bruise on her head, and crawls to the van's back door. She attempts to pry it open. To her surprise, the right door opens, and the light of the outside appears again to her.

Jaanika jumps out of the van and spies the woods and the road. She looks back and observes that the van has been in a terrible crash. Part of the van is seen to be smoldering, the doors have been severely dented, the window is smashed, and the vehicle is lying on its side. In a second, Jaanika decides to escape. She bolts in the direction of the woods as fast as she can with her hands cuffed. Her heart is racing, she is sweating, and her senses are acute. She continues to run faster and faster through the endless woods; she is on the edge of exhaustion. Her body wants to quit with every footstep, but she mentally continues past the pain. One hour passes. Jaanika spies only an occasional rabbit or bird. She looks around, and there appears to be no sign of people living in the area. She continues to walk swiftly through the woods. As night falls, Jaanika spots a small cottage, and no one appears to be home. She ventures into a small shed, which is unlocked, and spots some tools. She picks up a wire cutter. Jaanika recalls some of her KaPo training in Estonia. She quickly uses her acquired skill set, using the wire cutters to pick the lock and undo the handcuffs. She throws them to the ground when she is finished.

While concentrating on her task, Jaanika feels a burly man's hand put pressure on her neck, attempting to cut off her ability to breathe. She desperately gasps for air.

In a moment, her defenses kick into gear. She responds with a left elbow thrust into the assailant's stomach. The man, a bald, heavyset individual, removes his hands from her neck. Jaanika quickly spins around and lifts her foot. At full force, she launches a sidekick to the man's ribs that makes a direct hit and violently knocks him to the ground at full velocity. Jaanika lifts her fists, engages in several harsh punches to the man's face, and then hits his testicles numerous times. The man grimaces in pain and falls to the ground unconscious. His face is swelling and has several bruises, and blood is pouring from his mouth.

Jaanika looks through the man's pocket. She finds and removes a cell phone and runs away from the cottage, in the direction of the woods, at a full sprint. After several minutes, Jaanika stops momentarily. She inhales and exhales deeply, revealing she is worn out. She takes a piece of paper that contains a phone number from her shoe. She dials the number and hears several rings.

"Hello," a man answers in Estonian.

"I am here but a little lost," she urgently mentions while breathing heavily, anxiety emanating from her voice.

"Don't worry. I will find you by tracking your cell phone. It's easy to track your movements that way. Wait a minute. I just checked. You don't appear to be that far from Minsk. I will find you and pick you up shortly." Jaanika hangs up the cell.

Jaanika continues to walk at a brisk pace. She comes across a small village. She waits for twenty-five minutes and sees a car drive up.

"Jaanika!" the dark-haired man with glasses yells.

"Mikhail." Jaanika smiles and waves.

"Get in the car quick," Mikhail states from the driver's seat.

Jaanika walks to the small Russian car, opens the car door, and sits in the front seat. She hugs Mikhail.

"I will take you to Minsk and a place for you to hide for a couple of days," Mikhail informs.

"How were you able to find me so quickly?" Jaanika questions.

"You have to be adaptable to survive as a member of the opposition in Belarus. I have developed many computer-related skills to avoid detection by the KGB. Get rid of the cell phone. If I can track you through your cell phone, the KGB can, too," Mikhail says.

Jaanika throws the cell phone out the window as far as she can. The car speeds along the pock-marked roads of Minsk. After twenty minutes, Mikhail and Jaanika's car enters central Minsk. The car traverses a series of alleyways and unmarked side streets. They park the car. Mikhail and Jaanika get out and walk. They pass through a series of small alleyways until they arrive at a white building with a black "Y" prominently placed next to the door. Jaanika opens the door, walks down several flights of stairs, and arrives at a small bar, which has a sign stating in English "Propaganda." The place possesses a unique Belarus-like bohemian décor. There is music blaring from banned Belarus punk rock bands playing in the background, photographs of gritty New York City placed throughout the bar, and posters from the Radio Free Europe and Radio Freedom hang from the walls. Hipsters, with beards and casual clothes, populate the establishment. Some are chatting at small tables, while others are sitting at the bar and drinking their beer. The smell of cigarette smoke permeates the air.

Jaanika follows Mikhail, who heads into the back of the bar and walks into a small office.

"Aren't you afraid you will be caught here?" Jaanika questions. Jaanika appears exhausted and unnerved by her ordeal.

"They raid our place from time to time, but we are prepared. We can spot a KGB officer from a mile away. Only hipsters come here. We are a true banksy establishment. They would call this place an art bar in the United States," Mikhail remarks. He grins.

"I'm here with the teddy bear flight and also working with the Estonian KaPo, the Kaitsepolitsei, to obtain the information. I understand you have a source who possesses information for Estonian intelligence, the KaPo?" Jaanika asks.

"Yes, I know the person. He will provide me with the information, and I will transfer it to you. He's motivated by not having World War III in Europe," Mikhail mentions. He makes a call on his cell phone and speaks for several minutes.

"I will attempt to obtain the information as soon as possible," Mikhail says.

Mikhail shows Jaanika a small mattress, which is located at the back of the office. He sets it up with blankets and a pillow. "Jaanika you can sleep here tonight. I know you are probably exhausted from your escape from prison today. I have some clothes you might wear," Mikhail says. He leaves the room and returns with what appears to be a KGB uniform.

"Why this?" Jaanika questions. She appears confused.

"This is left over from a costume party I had at the bar. We are very ironic in the Free Belarus Movement. Plus, it looks good on you. Much better than prison clothes," Mikhail says.

"I think I lost my fashion sense in prison. Do you have Internet access here?" Jaanika asks.

"Here is my computer. Don't use it for too long, though," Mikhail says.

Jaanika boots up the computer and logs onto the web. She opens her email, which contains many unread messages. She spots an email from David Markoff. She reads it. She emails him using the encryption software on Mikhail's laptop. She writes, *I am in Minsk. My life is in danger. If I go back to prison, I will die. I will give you a contact person to get in touch with me. I need help getting out of the country. You are my only hope! Jaanika.*

Jaanika logs off the computer. She is elated beyond her dreams, as she breathes free for the first time. She sings the song of Estonian freedom to herself in a soft voice and slowly falls asleep.

Chapter 22

Tensions Rising

Helsinki, Finland

The prime minister's situation room is buzzing with activity. TV monitors are blaring with Russian and European TV stations' broadcasts. The latest pronouncement from the Kremlin-controlled media is aired. "Finnish nationalism is our greatest threat to Russia's national unity," the Russian Federal Security Service head announces. "Finland must be taught a lesson," he adds in a stern pronouncement.

Prime Minister Tarja Manninen enters the situation room with several members of her cabinet and the Finnish Council of Security in attendance. She looks quite dour and flashes a serious but friendly expression. Jarmo Bergstrom, the Finnish Security Intelligence Service director, is standing next to the table. He is wearing his usual blue suit, purple rimless glasses, and a blue tie.

Tarja nonverbally motions for Jarmo to sit down.

"The reason I am calling this meeting is evident. Russia is violating our airspace on a regular basis, Russian submarines are in the waters outside Helsinki, and the Russians are building up their forces on our eastern border," Tarja states. "It's time for us to revert to Cold War practices. We have to show resolve without starting something that may lead to a military exchange. Russia is clearly engaging in hybrid warfare now. They have even been pressuring us by sending tens of thousands of Syrian refugees living in their territory over our border. The new mantra of Russia's foreign ministry is *new rules or no rules.* They want to change the European Order now," Tarja adds.

"What did you have in mind?" Jarmo inquires.

"We will alert all our reserves in Finland of their roles if a war breaks out. This will demonstrate our determination to defend Finland. Do you have the list of Russian FSB and SVR agents currently working in Finland undercover?" Tarja asks.

"Yes, I have compiled a list of twenty names for you. I have highlighted the ones employed at the Russian embassy and the Russian news services," Jarmo answers.

"Do you have a list of CIA operatives currently working in Finland?" Tarja adds.

"I know of one agent," Jarmo says.

"Get me about twenty Russian names and one from the American CIA so the Russians get the message, but we can deny showing favorites. Russia's Federal Security Service and SVR think they own us presently," Tarja adds.

"Any idea what we should do if a crackdown in neighboring Karelia sends hundreds of thousands more refugees fleeing across the Finnish border?" Jarmo asks.

"Let's deal with one crisis at a time. I want to see the Russian reactions to our move first.

Let's not be so tense. My father survived the Russian–Finnish Winter War in 1939 and the continuation war of 1943." Tarja smiles.

"Yes, Prime Minister," Jarmo responds.

Tarja rises from her seat in the situation room and rushes to her next meeting. Jarmo sits at the desk and makes calls on his cell. "We have received the prime minister's orders. Let the operation start as soon as possible."

Chapter 23

SUPO Heat

David sits on a Finland Airlines flight traveling from Washington DC to Helsinki. He feels nervous anticipation. The CIA headquarters seems to trust him again. David no longer feels like a pariah who has been exiled to a desk job in a remote outpost, and he now possesses career prospects at the agency.

David takes his laptop out from his knapsack, which is lying below his airline seat. He places his laptop on the tray above his seat and proceeds to boot up his computer. David then logs on to the airline Internet connection. He proceeds to log on to his Department of State email and begins drafting a message: *Jake. I will return today. Let's meet as soon as possible. The HQ visit went well.*

The Boeing 757 lands at Helsinki-Vanta International Airport. David exits the airliner. He walks to Finnish immigration, where he patiently waits in line to enter the country.

David walks forward as he observes he is the next in line to be inspected. *"Terve."* The Finnish immigration officer nonverbally motions for David to present his passport.

David shows his diplomatic passport to the Finnish immigration officer. The woman scans David's passport into her computer system and runs his name through the Finnish immigration data systems.

"Welcome back to Finland," a Finnish immigration officer states and sports a friendly smile.

"*Kiitos*," David responds.

David walks through the immigration control into the interior of Helsinki-Vanta International Airport and heads to the baggage claim area.

After retrieving his bags, David is startled by the feeling of a hand pressing on his back. He quickly turns around and recognizes SUPO agent Pia Hjelt with two male officers standing behind her. They are wearing stern expressions.

David decides to appear as innocent as possible as the best way to defuse the situation. David presents a friendly smile. "Pia, are you traveling too?"

Pia seems solemn. "Actually, we are here to see you."

"Why me?" David responds and looks quite concerned.

"Can you come with us for a talk? I will lead the way," Pia asks. Her expression reveals her serious demeanor.

"This sounds like an offer that I can't refuse," David retorts. He shrugs and walks with the SUPO officers.

Pia leads David into an awaiting black Toyota Corolla. She sits in the backseat with David. The car drives from Vantaa to the center of Helsinki and to the SUPO office, which is located in central Helsinki at its Rantakatu 12 headquarters building. Pia, the two SUPO officers, and David exit the vehicle. They all enter the SUPO headquarters building, walk through a series of corridors, and arrive at a small room.

"Please sit down here for a moment," Pia informs and flashes a friendly smile. One SUPO officer sits down next to David in a chair several feet away. He is surprised to see Jake sitting in the corner of the room. David rises from his seat and approaches him.

Jakes appears a little worried. "I will not ask how the flight went, but hope you're OK."

David looks at Jake. "What are the charges that the SUPO are holding us on presently?" David asks.

"Performing inconsistent duties associated with our diplomatic status is the official charge at the moment. The SUPO might add other charges later," Jake says. He looks downtrodden.

"How long have you been here for?" David asks.

"Only a couple of hours. It has been boring, for the most part," Jake informs.

"Did you contact the embassy yet?" David inquires.

"Yes, I talked to the ambassador. He is sending someone to help us," Jake says.

Pia walks in and looks at David. "Please come with me."

"What about Jake?" David asks.

"We only want to talk to you," Pia explains and nonverbally gestures for David to walk in her direction.

They both walk into a small white room that contains a wooden table and several chairs. Pia smiles and offers David a seat. David proceeds to sit down in a small chair.

"So, how was your trip to Washington DC?" Pia sits down opposite David. Another SUPO official is quietly taking notes behind her.

"It started out nice, but the return flight does not seem to have ended up well," David observes.

"Nonsense. The SUPO and CIA are on good terms. You are among friends here. I am authorized to offer you a beverage or food if you want," Pia says.

David sits back in the chair. "I could use a nice swig of Finnish vodka," David remarks. He flashes a bemused smile.

"I think you know the SUPO has a strict non-alcohol policy. Our organization is not like the Russian FSB or SVR after all," Pia says.

David appears a little unnerved for a moment. He keeps his composure and plays the game. "I am only a State Department employee. I think you have detained the wrong person. You need to check your sources about this, Pia." David smiles slyly.

Pia opens a file lying in front of her. "OK, Mr. Consular Officer. Let me provide you with some information that may interest you. I know your cousin Jaanika is being held in Belarus by the Belarus KGB. If you want to cooperate with us, we will help you obtain information about her whereabouts. You can also help Finland in the process. We are in a tight situation with the Russians being quite aggressive currently. I want to let you know that we have to ask an American to leave Finland, as we are giving an exit notice to several of our Russian guests. "

David appears a little rattled. He regains his composure and is quiet for a moment. He thinks about his deceased wife and what game the SUPO is playing at this point. "Of course, any help for Jaanika would be appreciated by myself." David grins politely.

Pia looks at David. "You Americans talk a lot but are not always very sincere. Finns, as you might know, say little, but our words possess great meaning. Your future actions will determine if we can trust you." Pia pauses for a second. "In the meantime, I think we can work with you, David."

"What information can you provide about Jaanika? I am really worried about her," David inquires and looks quite interested.

"This will come in time. I will release you and Jake to the United States embassy officials, who are waiting outside," Pia says.

"Thanks for releasing me," David mentions. His expression reveals he is a little perturbed by the ordeal.

Pia motions for David to get up out of his seat. David walks out of the room and is escorted outside the facility to an awaiting car. He sees Jake in the car. He enters the black sedan.

"Nice to be free again," David remarks, takes a seat, and looks at Jake. "How you doing?"

"Well, I have some news for you. I have been ordered out of Finland by the Finnish government for performing duties inconsistent with my diplomatic position." Jake looks solemn.

"Lovely," David remarks. He rolls his eyes in disgust.

"You are going to be acting chief of station upon further word. You will see a cable going out from headquarters announcing your new role," Jake says.

"That's for the promotion. I am sure I'm receiving the same amount of pay after this promotion. Why do think the SUPO is applying the pressure now?" David asks.

"I think it probably has to do with the Finnish government ordering ten Russian officials out of the country. Our sources and intercepts reveal that there is a great deal of chatter among the Finnish intelligence and the political elite now associated with Russia's actions in Karelia," Jake says.

"I will talk to you after I get settled in," David remarks.

The black United States embassy sedan arrives in Kallio. David exits the car and walks into his apartment with his baggage in tow. He arrives at the front door of his apartment and spots an unmarked envelope.

David picks up the envelope. He brings it into his residence. He looks outside his apartment to see if there is any surveillance. He spots a black car down the street, which may be a sign that a SUPO team could be watching him. David walks to the kitchen and opens the envelope. He finds a piece of paper written in Spanish: *This is Lopez. I have been unable to contact you. I have information about our contact from Belarus. We can meet in Helsinki's Kaivopuisto Park. Send me a text when you get this and we can schedule a drop. I have fucking really good information for you. I expect appropriate payment!*

David calls Lopez. The phone rings several times. "Hello."

"Let's meet," David says.

"Sounds fucking nice to my ears," Lopez remarks.

"I'm being watched," David warns.

"*Yo comprendo,*" Lopez announces.

David changes into his running shoes. He takes his bundles of euros and places them inside his backpack. He feels ready for the trip to Kaivopuisto Park. He decides to deviate from normal tradecraft. Rather than schedule a drop point for an exchange of information, he decides to meet his source directly, though disguised and in an unusual manner. David figures the SUPO will not be expecting this, which will provide a chance for him to engage in the information exchange undetected. David knows this is extremely risky and that he might be detected.

David exits his apartment. He begins to jog and is wearing his backpack and running clothes. He runs around the Old Kallio church, down the hill, and in the direction of a big lake. He scans the area for signs of surveillance. David spots a tram about to leave in the direction of Kaivopuisto and jumps on at the last minute. He travels south for several minutes and arrives near the diplomatic area of Helsinki. David jumps off the tram and runs in the direction of the Baltic Sea. He enters a jogging trail and follows it through the park. He looks around.

In the distance appears another runner. He appears rather odd-looking with his long hair, tattoos, and brawny shoulders. As he comes closer, it appears that the runner is Lopez. David continues to jog and approaches Lopez as he continues running along the trail that follows the Baltic Sea.

"Nice day, *mi amigo!*" Lopez smiles. He looks a little winded as he runs.

"You too," David retorts.

Both jog at a slow pace.

"I have obtained some good information for you. Turns out that the two operatives have arrived in Helsinki. They appear to be here to carry out an operation. Their last names are Mikhailovich and Serkin. They are in Helsinki now. I have their location and have placed the details on this thumb drive. I tried to call you a couple of times. You have been incognito," Lopez remarks. He slips the thumb drive into David's pocket.

David smiles and remarks in Spanish, "That's information worth paying for." He clandestinely hands Lopez the envelope.

"*Adios.*" Lopez smiles.

David continues to run, and his phone vibrates. He looks at his phone and views a text message: *Please come to the St. Petersburg Cellar. We are having a meeting of sorts. Cliff Armstrong.*

David checks the location of St. Petersburg Cellar on his phone. He hails a cab via his smartphone app. One soon arrives.

"Please take me to the café at 26 Mannerheim Katu," David states.

"*Joo*," the Finnish driver says.

The car drives through the beautiful Swedish 19th century–style neighborhood that borders the Baltic Sea. He arrives at a restaurant with a small brick façade. "*Tassa*. St. Petersburg's Cellar."

"*Kiitos*," David remarks. He gives the taxi driver a tip.

He gets out of the car and walks to the front door of the business. A tall Slavic man in dark glasses guards the door and greets David.

"What do you want?" he remarks in Russian-accented English.

"I'm here to see Cliff Armstrong. My name is David Markoff," David says.

The man takes his cell phone out of his pocket, dials a number, and mentions David's name.

He opens the door. "Here," he orders in Russian.

David walks inside and is immediately surrounded by the sounds of the famous Soviet-Russian musician Vladimir Visockiy singing. He continues to walk into the restaurant and spots ten men and several Russian women in the club. They are all drinking and dressed in high style.

Cliff Armstrong's voice can be heard. "*Privet*, David. Welcome to our club. We celebrate Russian culture here. Our group is called the Siloviki"

David feels a chill go down his spine. "It's good to see you, Cliff. The Siloviki. . . your group left me notes. Why are you watching me?" David asks. David appears miffed.

"David, we only invite a select few to the club. We have made sure you are worthy of membership. We have vetted you. We trust you, as you are from the Russian countryside. You can be part of our new Russian project," Cliff states enthusiastically.

David wonders, *Is this a trap? Are the Siloviki in fact part of the Russian SVR or could the CIA be testing his loyalty? Was the CIA mission in DC only a ruse?* His paranoia continues to build as the seeds of doubt germinate within his mind. "I am glad you thought of me. I would like to experience your organization first before joining. I hope that is alright with you," David replies.

"Sit down and join us in a vodka toast," Cliff mentions and slaps David on the back.

"I would be honored," David responds and flashes a friendly smile.

Cliff sits down at the bar and hands David a vodka shot.

"Have you been attending many ice hockey games lately?" David questions.

"Not many. My diplomatic duties and Finnish–US relations have kept me busy lately," Cliff says.

"I heard you were detained by the SUPO. Hope that was not too unpleasant?" Cliff asks. He looks a little concerned.

"I will survive. I'm having a little problem that you may be able to assist me with. The KGB is holding my cousin, Jaanika Olson, in Belarus. Perhaps you can help? Do you have any contacts in Belarus?" David asks.

"I will look into it and see what I can do," Cliff remarks.

A tall, dark man with a Slavic complexion, who is wearing an extremely expensive suit, walks up to Cliff. Cliff introduces him. "David, I would like you to meet Dmitry, who owns Helsinki's professional ice hockey team, Jokerit. He is very influential. I think he is the real brains behind Russian President Vladimirovich." Cliff laughs.

"You are too kind. I'm a simple businessman." Dmitry smiles and shakes David's hand.

"So, I heard you're originally from Russian Karelia?" Dmitry asks. He flashes a polite smile.

"Yes. I was born in Russia," David remarks. He wonders if Dmitry is a Russian SVR agent. He decides to proceed with extreme caution.

"Soon all of Karelia, including the Finnish area, will be in Russian hands. We need people to build the new Russia. You should come back to the motherland," Dmitry remarks in Russian.

"I appreciate your offer. I am too involved in my assignment now to think about the new Russia or other issues for that matter," David says.

"Don't ever turn down a *Siloviki*" Cliff warns, smiles, and chuckles a little. "He is former FSB, you know. You don't want to end up dead in a hotel room."

"Think about it," Dmitry says. He motions for several more drinks to be served at the table.

"To a future Siloviki member." Cliff and Dmitry lift their glasses in a toast.

David drinks his cocktail and smiles. He flashes a friendly smile to Cliff.

"If you work for the CIA, we will kill you," Cliff whispers into David's ear in a harsh tone.

David is a little startled and surprised by the ambassador's statement. His eyes open wide. He responds, "OK."

David drinks with Cliff and Dmitry into the late hours of the night and returns home extremely paranoid. He knows that the stakes are high in the spy game, but he is not sure which side the United States ambassador is on at this point. Ambassador Armstrong is a prominent political figure in the United States, and David knows that he must possess evidence before making any accusations against him.

Chapter 24

A Vyborg Mystery

On a rare summer day, the unusually beautiful weather beckons David to sit at one of the outdoor cafés that exist in abundance in the Kallio section of Helsinki. David is seated at a small table, after having just completed a 10K run around the neighborhood, and appears to be enjoying his exile from Washington DC. His cup of coffee is lying in front of him as he is intently focused on playing the latest Finnish game application that he has downloaded onto his smart device. David appears momentarily frustrated by his failure to progress to the next level in the game, to the point of almost spilling his coffee.

"Drasyote!" an unknown voice states in Russian.

David's concentration is diverted to the sound of the Russian greeting. He looks up and sees Yuri standing in front of him. He is wearing a jeans jacket, blue pants, and a white shirt.

"I'm surprised to see you here. I did not realize you visit Kallio. Is this a big hangout for people working at the Russian embassy?" David says. He looks at Yuri.

"Actually, I'm here to follow up on our conversation we had in Moscow. You indicated that you were interested in information about the company Interex Oy. I took the time to run down all the information for you and have placed it inside a folder," Yuri says. He flashes a friendly smile.

"Sit down," David responds. He nonverbally motions for Yuri to sit in the vacant seat across from the table.

"Thank you." Yuri sits down in the chair and takes out a folder from his briefcase.

"So, what do you know about Interex exactly?" David asks. He appears quite interested in Yuri's information.

"The firm has an office in Vyborg in Karelia and St. Petersburg. It's involved with the transportation of truck freight. The company operates trucking routes between Helsinki and St. Petersburg, Russia. Here is their address in Vyborg. I hope this assists your family-related issue."

"Thank you for your help," David says. He smiles politely.

"Do you plan to travel to Vyborg or St. Petersburg? I can help you with the trip if you want,"

Yuri adds. He passes a folder containing the company information across the table.

"I might need some assistance later. I will contact you if I need any help." David surmises that he has to keep all his options open but not let the Russian SVR know he might visit Russia. He wonders what the true motivations of Russian intelligence are for providing the assistance, other than the fact that they want to recruit him as a double agent. *Is this a trap?* David wonders.

"In return, I would love to have you join me at an event at the Russian embassy," Yuri suggests. He flashes a polite smile.

"Sure. If I have time, I will attend. Please send me the information," David says.

"Thank you for your assistance. Please excuse me for leaving so quickly, but I have an appointment," David shakes Yuri's hand and walks away.

He travels to his office at the United States embassy. He opens his backpack, takes out the folder, and reviews all the information that Yuri has provided. He sees a summary of the company, the picture of a building located in Vyborg, and all the information about Vyborg, a small town in Russia.

David decides to use his investigate skills and visit the company. David knows there is one obstacle to his investigation. He must request permission for the operation from CIA headquarters with a cable.

***TO: CIA HQ From: Helsinki Station**, Title: **Operation Vyborg Request.** I am requesting permission to travel to Vyborg for an operation associated with the company Interex Oy, which may have been associated with the assassination attempt on a CIA agent in Finland. I have informed the Moscow station of my operation. This operation will hope to undercover the true nature of Interex and find more information about the source of an operation against a CIA agent that took place in Finland.*

David waits for the approval. He omits his interaction with the Russian embassy official for the meantime. *The answer to what happened to my wife's remains lie in Vyborg, Russia,* David surmises. The doubt of not knowing what happened to his wife's remains is tearing him up inside and wreaking havoc on his consciousness.

Chapter 25

The Helsinki KGB Operation

"1, 23, 7, 15, and 19" boom out in a monotone female Russian voice from a small black digital radio that possesses an antenna that is fully deployed. KGB Officer Ivan Mikhailovich sits within a small apartment in Helsinki listening closely to the radio's speaker, which amplifies the shortwave broadcast. The antiquated whistles and static of shortwave radio transmissions are the only way to ensure security in the age of insecure digital communication. Mikhailovich writes the numbers down on a pad of paper. Once the broadcast concludes, Mikhailovich looks at the deciphering key lying on the table, which reveals the true meaning of the coded letters.

"Vladimir, how are you feeling?" Mikhailovich asks. He is busily writing on a small pad of paper lying in front of him.

"Good. I'm a little tense at the moment. This is my first operation, and I want it to start as soon as possible," Vladimir responds and nervously peers outside the apartment's window. He then paces around the room as if he is letting off pent-up energy.

"Relax. Staying calm and under control is the most important part of the job. If you become nervous, you will stick out more here, and people will become suspicious," Mikhailovich lectures. He shakes his head a little in disgust at Vladimir's inexperience.

Mikhailovich begins to decipher the message from the KGB headquarters in Minsk and writes the true meaning on a small piece of paper lying next to him. Mikhailovich completes deciphering the message. He sits in the back of his seat and reads it: *Operation Helsinki please standby. Be ready to engage several targets, which will be provided to you soon.*

Vladimir stands at the other end of the room. He picks up a pistol and begins cleaning the barrel and wiping the gun clean.

"What is our plan? When do we go into action?" Vladimir inquires, looking a little nervous.

"Vladimir, this is a waiting game. We have to avoid any possibility of exposure to the SUPO or the CIA. We will first conduct casing of the operation's targets. We will practice the operation. Then, we must design an exit plan," Mikhailovich says.

"What sport did you play at university?" Mikhailovich inquires. He looks up from his paper and at Vladimir, who is now standing next to the window.

"We had a hockey rink built in our small town. I am from Uzda. I played forward on our team,"

Vladimir responds. He peers out the apartment window.

"I played hockey a little but studied chess, too. The game we are playing now requires the skill set of chess. We have to know when to strike and when to hold back," Mikhailovich adds.

"In hockey, you have all that. You study your goalie, learn his weakness, and design a strategy of where to shoot the puck. It's also about strategy," Vladimir states in protest.

"I hope you have learned, as this is a game of life and death now," Mikhailovich says. "Can you go shopping? We need some food. Then, I need you to take the pictures of some possible targets," Mikhailovich asks.

"Yes, sir," Vladimir remarks. He seems excited to leave the apartment.

Vladimir puts down his automatic weapon and pistol and gently wraps them in protective cloth. He puts on his leather jacket. He opens the door and looks left and right. He walks out of the apartment onto the main street in Helsinki. He nonchalantly strides down several blocks on his way to a local market in Helsinki called Kioski.

As he walks, Vladimir is momentarily distracted and stares at several strikingly beautiful blond-haired Finnish women walking by the market and talking on their cell phones. He continues to walk and peer at the women and accidentally bumps into a tall, burly, long-haired, tattooed man in a leather jacket.

"Watch yourself, motherfucker!" Lopez growls in Finnish and flashes an intimidating stare.

Vladimir stares menacingly at Lopez for a moment and then continues to walk to the grocery store.

Lopez continues to track Vladimir at a distance and sees that he has entered the grocery store. He is playing a waiting game that only a professional has mastered.

Chapter 26

David sits at his desk inside his secured office, which is located within the United States embassy. He types on his keyboard: ***Helsinki Operations Cable, Limited Dissemination to CIA Headquarters.*** *This is Helsinki Acting Chief of Station Markoff. Jake has departed Finland. I am requesting permission to assist American national Jaanika Olson to gain her release from KGB custody in Belarus. Our US embassy in Minsk is closed and can't assist. I will need cash and operational assistance to launch a rescue operation. I am reporting that I have uncovered a group in Helsinki called the Siloviki. Several members appear to be former Russian intelligence officers. I will meet with MINSK EYES and forward my report as requested by CIA headquarters.*

David receives a text on his smartphone: *We need a good sauna. Pia.* He knows that is the signal to meet for an intelligence exchange with the SUPO.

David walks out of the office and then out of the United States embassy. He takes the tram to Kallio. He exits the tram and walks through a series of side streets and arrives at Kaupunki Sauna, a small, nondescript establishment with a wood-burning sauna. David enters the establishment, pays the entry fee, changes clothes, and walks into the wood-burning sauna, where he sees Pia wearing a towel. There is a man in the sauna whom David does not recognize. When the man leaves, David speaks.

"*Terve*, David," Pia remarks. "Nice to see you. I have information about your cousin." Pia smiles.

"Is she OK?" David asks. He appears concerned.

"She has escaped from KGB custody. We have a source in the Belarus government who stated that her vehicle crashed when she was being transported to a court hearing. She was going to be charged with assisting terroristic acts for her activities associated with the teddy bear bombing of Belarus and attempting to escape from prison."

"Do you know where she is located currently?" David asks.

"I know the KGB is searching for her. That is all I can tell you at this point. I have a contact in the Belarus opposition. Our intelligence sources can't provide a complete picture of the situation at the moment," Pia says.

"How confident are you of this source? Can I task him or her for further questioning?" David inquires.

"You must have worked as an analyst. Only an analyst would ask those questions. Very well. Our assessment is that he has a good reporting history in the past. We keep our sources clandestine inside SUPO. I can give you the name and email address of an opposition activist. His name is Mikhail. He may be able to assist you with information," Pia says. She smiles.

"What information can you provide me?" Pia takes out a pad and paper and begins to write.

"Well, there may be some Belarus operatives in Helsinki. I don't know why they are here. They may want to kill someone or have landed in Finland for other purposes. My information is sketchy at this point," David mentions.

"Do you have names and locations?" Pia questions. She looks quite concerned.

"Not yet," David responds. David decides not to provide all the information to the SUPO yet. He wants to keep the information about Jaanika flowing but not show all he knows and does not know. This is good spy tradecraft.

"Get me more information about their location and possible targets," Pia says.

"I will try. A nice restaurant may be a better location next time. Wear a cute Finnish-designed dress also," David smiles slyly.

"Please keep the intelligence flowing, and you will be on good terms with the SUPO. You have a nice smile also," Pia remarks. She appears a little amused.

David walks out of the sauna and changes into his street clothes in the locker room. He walks to the subway. David looks at his encrypted smartphone and sees a message: *Helsinki calling.* David replies on his phone: *Bear Park in Kallio. 1:00 p.m. Know the contact phrase.*

David walks out of his apartment into a rainy summer day in Helsinki. He loads his gun and places it under his coat. He enters Bear Park, which is located near the iconic Kallio Church. The park possesses a prominent statue of a large bear. He walks to a small bench and sits down. He is strategically located to spot any surveillance. While sitting, David ponders the fate of Jaanika and how he can use his meeting to his advantage. David knows never to trust anyone and to always remain skeptical of any person's true motivations.

A few minutes later, a Slavic-looking man in his thirties, who is wearing a dark coat, walks to the bench and sits behind David. Mikhailovich takes out a cigarette from his jacket, lights it, and extinguishes the match. He looks around to spot any possible surveillance. "Do you know of any good coffee places in Kallio?" he asks. "I only know of those located in Washington DC," David responds. *It must be Mikhailovich*, David thinks to himself.

"Welcome to Finland," David whispers. David takes out a Finnish newspaper and pretends to peruse different sections of the paper. David is wary. He is aware of the ruthless reputation of the Belarus KGB. He assesses that they are a good but very regimented security service. Their intelligence capabilities are limited. David expects few surprises from the KGB, but he is still on guard when dealing with them. Never underestimating anyone is good tradecraft for the intelligence world.

"I'm here on a mission. I have contacted you as I need your support," Mikhailovich quietly informs.

"What is your mission in Finland specifically?" David asks. David does not want to give an indication that he knows Mikhailovich's activity. He is playing the spy game and knows that you should never show your real intentions and always keep everyone guessing about what you know and don't know.

"We have to take out several targets here on orders from the Belarus government. I want support from you. I'm working in Belarus to form a new government and remove the Russian influence. Belarus will not survive as an independent state for long. Russian government influence is taking over rapidly. Can I count on your support?" Mikhailovich asks.

"Whom are you taking out?" David asks. He continues to peer at his newspaper.

"Several high-ranking targets," Mikhailovich responds. He takes a cigarette, puts it to his lips, and takes a puff. He sits there with a cigarette in hand.

"Can you provide any more detailed information?" David whispers.

"If I receive your support, you will get some information. I don't trust you, so come back soon," Mikhailovich says. He takes another puff of his cigarette.

"What will we obtain in return?" David whispers.

Mikhailovich takes another puff of his cigarette. "You can count on a friend in power in Belarus. I hear the United States and NATO need friends right now," Mikhailovich says.

"Who will carry out the hit?" David asks. He casually turns the page of the newspaper.

"I am here with another agent," Mikhailovich says.

"How can I trust you?" David inquiries. He is trying to gauge Mikhailovich's reaction. He knows the answer. The spy game is to play all angles to assess the credibility of your source.

"The Russian SVR is watching you. Should they find out that I met with you, I am a dead man," Mikhailovich says. He drops the cigarette to the ground and extinguishes it by placing his foot on the burning butt.

"I will get back to you with our decision," David says.

"Do it soon. All deals are off if I don't hear from you," Mikhailovich warns.

David gets up from the bench in Bear Park. He walks back to the United States embassy. He walks into his office. He logs onto the computer and checks his classified email.

The message reads, ***CIA Headquarters Cable to Helsinki Station***, ***MINSK EYES***, Permission to *assist Jaanika Olson is denied. Please assist Mikhailovich at all costs. Finnish interests are not the issue in the case. He is a high-value source.* David is stunned by this decision. He can't believe that they will not allow him to help a United States citizen.

David logs onto his personnel email: *Let's meet in Minsk. I can help with Jaanika. Send me a date and time. Mikhail.*

David feels conflicted. He wants to be loyal to the CIA but feels he has a mission greater than himself. He owes it to Terhi. Jaanika Olson's life remains in the balance. He will not fail his family again. David knows that he must make a decision that will impact his future. He wonders if he can trust Mikhail and the odds of succeeding in saving Jaanika. He knows that he must make an important decision. David has to commit himself to saving Jaanika or to his career in the CIA. He can't stay on the fence anymore.

Chapter 27

Mission Belarus

At 7:00 a.m., David awakens and rises from bed. The midsummer sun can be seen less within his apartment. This is a sign that the short Nordic summer is clearly on the wane, and winter can be felt to be fast approaching by the rapidly shortening hours of daylight.

With a sense of mission and rightness of purpose, David retrieves all his false passports, several thousand in euros and Russian rubles, a dissembled gun, and several SIM cards for cell phones from his safe, which he has hidden underneath his bed. He places all his true identity documents inside a safe located in his apartment and fills two duffle bags with the equipment and materials to carry out his operation. He has decided to break with the CIA, travel to Belarus, and assist his cousin Jaanika Olson.

David's cell phone rings. The number does not appear on the screen, but he answers it. He places the cell phone next to his ear. "Hello."

"This is Pia. Time for another sauna."

"Can you meet me in Vantaa near the airport?" David asks.

"Sure. Let's meet at the airport's new sauna instead. It might be a better venue," Pia says.

"I will be there," David says.

"*Hei Hei*," Pia remarks. She hangs up the phone.

David places his phone within his pocket and exits his apartment. He looks for signs of any surveillance. Cars with people sitting inside watching, a person whom he has seen before, or anything out of the ordinary are possible indicators in David's mind. He sees nothing, to his relief, and continues on his journey to Helsinki's international airport.

David walks to the tram stop, waits for several minutes, and boards a tram heading in the direction of Helsinki City Center. After reaching downtown Helsinki, David boards a bus which will transport him to Helsinki-Vantaa's international departures terminal. He is quiet and apprehensive as he travels. His knows his break with the CIA will change his life. He will be on the run now and a wanted former CIA official. David knows he is not an ordinary fugitive and will be deemed to be a high-value target.

After arriving at the airport, David walks to a section of the airport that has a sign marked

"Communal Sauna and Lounge," which is located within the main terminal. He pays a fee at the front desk and receives a key and a towel. He enters the sauna's locker room, changes into sauna-appropriate clothing, and enters the communal unisex sauna. He sits down on one of the wood benches. Pia enters the heated room and walks into the sauna. She proceeds to sit next to David.

They say nothing for several minutes. Several strangers present in the sauna leave the room. Both Pia and David are left alone inside the hot wooden sauna interior.

"*Terve*." Pia smiles. She combs her hair.

"Hope you don't mind another sauna-connected meeting. I need a hot sauna before departing on a dangerous mission." David flashes a friendly smile. He is sweating and wearing only a towel but decides it is not hot enough. He takes a bucket of water with a scoop and flings the water toward the hot sauna, which is located in the corner of the room. The water strikes the sauna and instantly vaporizes. This causes a mist that seems to smack David and Pia in the face. Both Pia and David begin to sweat profusely, as perspiration streams down their faces and bodies.

"*Niin*," Pia remarks. She flashes a friendly smile.

David appears serious. "I have to leave for Belarus. I have no other choice. Jaanika is in trouble, and the United States government will not allow me to assist her. I know where she is located now. I need to go," David says.

"David, are you sure you know what you're doing?" Pia questions. She looks concerned. She proceeds to wipe her face with a towel.

"With Belarus, I kind of feel as though I am going back to the 1980s and trying to break into the Soviet Union," David remarks. He pauses in thought for a moment. "Pia, you know you are never certain in the intelligence business but only possess a degree of confidence about any decision you make. My plan is to head back to Finland when the mission in complete. The border between Russia and Belarus is less stringently patrolled, and I am hoping it will be easy to cross and give me a chance to succeed. I'm doing this for Terhi and my family. I know Terhi is with me in spirit on this mission. I am not going to fail this time," David declares. He appears quite emotional. "Pia, I trust you for some reason. Maybe it's because the Finns are very honest by nature."

"*Joo*," Pia responds. She flashes a friendly smile.

"So, do you trust Mikhail?" David inquires. He appears a little concerned.

"David, he is a real opposition activist. I know of his blog and that he has been jailed many times demonstrating against the Belarus government. I am confident he will assist you. I have to be honest with you, David. The odds are against you to succeed in your mission. The Belarus KBG is aware of your work for the CIA, as they are deeply integrated with Russian intelligence. Honestly, I don't think risking your life in Belarus will bring back your wife," Pia says.

"You may be right. I still have to make an attempt to rescue Jaanika. She is a member of my family," David mutters.

David reaches into a small pale of water lying next to him. He throws another scoop full of water at the hot sauna located in the corner of the room. The steam rises from the sauna after the water strikes the hot coils.

Pia reaches into a pouch that she has lying next to her and takes out a small box. She opens the box and takes out a silver chain and cross. "David. I have a present for you. Here is a good-luck charm. I hope it will help you succeed. If you need anything, let me know," Pia remarks. She hands the old Nordic cross necklace to David.

David looks at the charm for a moment and puts it around his neck. "*Kiitos*," David says.

Pia gets up from the bench in the sauna. They embrace. David looks into Pia's blue eyes.

"Life is just a series of fateful decisions. Perhaps it's the best alternative in a situation where there are few options. Only time will tell," David says.

"*Niin,*" Pia says.

David hugs Pia. He exits the sauna, walks into the changing room, and changes into his street clothes. He walks up to the airline counter in the airport and approaches a woman who is standing at Poland's National Airlines desk.

"May I help you?" she questions.

"My name is Jason Smith. I am traveling to Poland," David says. He takes out his passport and presents it to the woman for inspection.

The woman working at the counter scans his passport and types in the name. "Here is your ticket to Warsaw. Have a good flight, Mr. Smith." She flashes a businesslike smile.

"Thanks," David remarks. He retrieves his passport and places it into his pocket.

David walks to the gate and boards the airliner. Several hours later, the airliner lands in Warsaw,

Poland. David walks off the flight. He walks through immigration and into the international airport, where he spots the lines for cabs. He approaches a cab and opens the back door. He proceeds to take a seat in the back of the cab.

"You speak English?" David questions.

"Yes," the taxi driver says, looking to the backseat of the car.

"Can you take me to Warsaw's central bus station?" David asks.

"Sure," the driver quips as the car begins to accelerate.

The taxi travels from the airport into the downtown area of the capital.

"So, where are you traveling to?" The taxi driver inquires.

"I am heading to Belarus," David answers.

"Why would you go there? Are you interested in some cheap hookers?" the driver asks. He chuckles a little.

"They have those in Minsk? I am visiting a friend who teaches English at one of the schools located in the city." David attempts to sound convincing with his cover story.

"Enjoy your stay. Crime is very rare in Minsk, but the Belarus KGB can be a pain to deal with when you cross the border," the Polish cab driver says.

"Thanks for the advice," David states.

The cab arrives at the bus station. David pays the taxi driver and takes his bags with him inside the station.

David presents a Russian passport, buys a ticket on "Interconnect Lines," and sits down. He notices nothing out of the ordinary. *No sign of the CIA or KGB at this point,* he thinks to himself. He checks his duffle bags and finds that all his tools are in order. He downloads a map of Minsk/Belarus and its suburbs onto his smartphone.

After several hours, David boards the bus and takes a seat in the middle of the bus to allow for a good vantage point, which will enable him to detect any possible surveillance. The bus pulls out of the station and drives through downtown Warsaw, which is bustling with traffic. He scans the passengers for any signs of covert intelligence activity. After a quick survey of the bus passengers, he is relieved to see nothing out of the ordinary.

The bus continues on its journey to Belarus, and David falls asleep as it travels away from Warsaw and through various small towns en route to the Belarus border.

At 7:00 p.m., the bus arrives at the Belarus–Polish border and stops. David keeps clam, as he knows Belarus immigration will conduct a passport check. After fifteen minutes, several heavyset men wearing gray uniforms and carrying guns on their sides board the bus. The inspection of all passengers aboard the bus begins with an interrogation of all passengers attempting to enter Belarus. One border guard official walks from passenger to passenger asking the usual questions in a sharp, unfriendly manner.

"Name, reason for traveling, and your visa," the officer demands.

David feels a little nervous. He spots an officer talking to a passenger in the row in front of him. The man is middle-aged.

"What is your name?" the officer asks.

"Dmitry Kaleova," the man responds.

"Can I see your passport?" the officer asks.

"Yes," the man says.

The officer looks at the passport for a minute. "You are being arrested for smuggling illegal goods." The Belarus immigration officer orders. He reaches out and grabs the man's arms. He places the cuffs on his hands and walks him off the bus.

Another border guard approaches David's seat. David appears calm but is sweating a little.

"Passport," the border guard barks in Russian.

David presents it to the guard. The Belarus border guard looks at him suspiciously. "There is a problem," the border guard says. He hands the passport back to David.

"What exactly?" David inquires. David looks at his passport intently. He seems a bit puzzled for a moment. He realizes what is actually occurring.

"There is a defect within your passport. You will need to obtain a new one," the Belarus guard says.

David looks at the passport again. He pauses for second to think of his next move. An idea flashes within his mind. "I see the defect. I am so sorry. I will get that fixed. Maybe this will make up for the problem." David reaches into his pocket and pulls out several euro notes. He then slips two hundred euro notes into the guard's hand.

The guard looks at the euros, places them into his pocket, and smiles. "Your passport seems OK now."

"Thank you, sir," David says. He smiles politely.

The guard walks away from David's seat and moves on to inspect the next passenger. Several minutes later, the Belarus border guards exit the bus. The bus driver announces in Polish, "We will now enter Belarus. Our next stop is Minsk." The bus begins to accelerate down the road and travels east in the direction of the Belarus capital.

At 9:00 p.m., David's bus arrives in Minsk. David walks off the bus with his knapsacks in tow. He heads in the direction of a local youth hostel, which David knows is less likely to be monitored by the KGB than the local hotels. David walks to the Minsk subway and takes it near Minsk Technical University. He exits the subway and spots a small, dilapidated building marked "Hostel." It is obvious by the oddly shaped interior that it was built during Soviet Communism. David enters the building and approaches the front desk.

"How can I help you?" a dark-haired female in her twenties inquires in Russian.

"*Privet*! I need a place for the night," David responds in Russian. She flashes a friendly smile.

"Name?" the tall woman standing at the front desk asks.

"Boris Ivanovich," David replies.

"Where are you from?" she adds. She looks quite interested.

"Vyborg, Russia. It's located in Russian Karelia. Here is my Russian passport," David says. David feels a little nervous, as the woman may be a KGB informant.

The woman views David's passport for a moment. "Russian Karelia. We rarely have visitors from that area. The room will be 200 rubles." She smiles and gives David's passport back to him.

David pays the woman.

"Hope your stay is enjoyable," the woman responds and hands him the key to the room.

David walks up several flights of stairs to his room. He enters the bathroom, tears up the United States passport he used to enter the country, and proceeds to flush it down the toilet. David is now Boris Ivanovich and is from Vyborg in Russian Karelia. His cover story is that he is visiting Minsk on holiday. David assumes that his Slavic looks and Russian language abilities will be the key to the success of his mission. He proceeds to open his knapsacks, takes out all the parts of his gun, and begins to assemble it. He takes out ammunition, a map of Belarus, and a map of the Belarus–Russian border.

David turns on the TV and watches a Belarus NTV Broadcast. An old Soviet World War film is playing. After several minutes, a woman newscaster appears on the screen. She announces in Russian, "The Russian government has warned Finland against their revanchist policies in Karelia. In a statement, President Vladimirovich has suggested that such a country deserves no longer to be independent. He warns Finland not to intervene in Karelia and the internal affairs of Russia."

David walks away from the TV and unpacks his clothes. He looks out the window suspiciously and does not observe any surveillance. He is satisfied that all is well. David proceeds to turn off the TV. He proceeds to go to sleep. Several hours later, David is awaken by a loud pounding on his front door. He awakes with his heart pumping with fear. His fight or flight response springs into action. He is not sure what to do and is puzzled, as he did not see any sign of the KGB. David quietly rises from his bed and slowly approaches the door as the loud banging on his door continues unabated. David glances through a peephole in the door outside and immediately recognizes a drunk Belarus woman. She has black hair, a small nose and red cheeks, and she is wearing a gown.

David feels a sense of relief and opens the door. "Can I help you?" he states in Russian.

"I am looking for my boyfriend. You don't look like him," the drunken, black-haired woman mumbles.

"He is not here, though. I think you're mistaken," David says.

"Oh." The intoxicated Russian-speaking woman slowly staggers away from David's door.

David closes the door and locks it securely. He goes back to his bed, a little shaken, and returns to sleep.

At 8:00 a.m., David awakens and grabs his knapsacks and his Russian passport. He looks outside from his bedroom window. He sees nothing out of the ordinary. David looks at his phone and notices that he has received an email. He opens it: *This is Mikhail. Welcome to Belarus. The party will begin at Propaganda bar. Bring the beer.*

He walks out of the youth hotel and heads in the direction of Propaganda bar. David begins to walk the streets of Minsk. An unidentified man, who is wearing a distinctive KGB uniform, approaches David from behind. David spots the KGB officer and wonders what to do. He remembers his training. He stays calm and appears normal. He decides to risk an encounter.

"Mister, I need to see your papers?" the KGB officer inquires in a surly tone.

"I am more than happy to provide you my passport. Here it is," David responds in Karelian-accented Russian. He hands the passport to the KGB officer.

"Did you register in Belarus as required for all foreigners?" the officer asks. He seems quite dour.

"No, you see I'm a Russian citizen visiting Belarus. I did not think I was required to register. I have some nice vodka if you want for my Belarus neighbor. I hope this will make up for my error." David smiles.

"No need." He looks at David's passport, intently examining his picture and the visas issued inside his passport.

"Your reason for visiting Belarus?" the officer asks. He appears to be gauging David's response.

"I'm seeking treatment for my back at a spa here." David smiles. David points to his spine to make his point known.

"OK, I understand. Have a good time with the women here. The brothels can be dangerous, so be careful." The officer smiles, hands David his passport, and appears to walk away.

Another close call, David thinks to himself. David feels a little rattled but proceeds to walk through Minsk, heads through a number of alleyways, and approaches a white building with a door that possesses a unique Belarus "Y" on top of it. This is the symbol of the Belarus resistance. The opposition shows its defiance against the Russification of the country by using the Belarusian alphabet.

David knocks on the door and looks both ways to assure himself that he is not being watched. A young man in his twenties, who is wearing hipster-like dress and sporting a goatee, answers the door.

"I am looking for Mikhail," David says.

The man looks at him. "What took you so long? We have been waiting for you. I thought you Americans valued being on time."

"I had some KGB-related issues that delayed me." David grins slyly.

"OK, come inside." The young man flashes a friendly smile. He points David in the direction to follow.

David walks down several flights of stairs and emerges in a room that is a bar; it is very quiet, and the lights are dimmed. "Are you under the hood?" a man in a trench coat and hat asks. He appears out of the shadows.

"What do you mean?" David questions. He appears confused.

"We in the Belarus opposition have a term for being under surveillance by the KGB. It is called being under the hood," Mikhail says.

"To the best of my knowledge, no," David retorts. "I am David Markoff. I have come here from the American embassy in Helsinki to rescue Jaanika. I am Jaanika's cousin," David says.

"I think Jaanika has freed herself at this point. I work with the Belarus opposition. You will only know me as Mikhail. We are working in dangerous territory, as we are hiding from the authorities," Mikhail quips.

"Is Jaanika in good health?" David questions. He looks concerned.

Jaanika walks into the room in KGB attire and recognizes David. He notices that she has scars and bruises marking her face.

"I have not seen you in a long time. You received my email," Jaanika says. She walks up to David and hugs him. To David, it feels like he is touching Terhi again.

"I love the KGB garb," David remarks. "It is very Soviet retro chic," David adds and smiles warmly.

"This is the perfect disguise," Jaanika states. Her smile reveals her newfound happiness at being out of jail.

"How are you feeling?" David inquires. "Have you been seen by a doctor?" He looks concerned.

"I'm alive and OK. I have not seen a doctor yet," Jaanika says.

"What is your next move?" David asks. He looks at Mikhail, hoping for details.

"We need to leave Belarus as soon as possible. The authorities are searching for Jaanika. I think the search for her may be cooling down a little and we can make an attempt now," Mikhail says.

"I would suggest heading to Russia. The border is lightly controlled, and crossing the border into Estonia might be easier than crossing into Lithuania, Latvia, or Finland," David remarks.

"Sounds good to me. I am ready to make an attempt," Mikhail responds.

"I have brought several fake passports and other materials for the trip," David informs.

"Jaanika, are you ready to leave?" David questions.

"*Joo*," Jaanika retorts.

"I can hear you have become more Finnish since I last saw you in Minnesota," David remarks. He grins happily.

David, Mikhail, and Jaanika enter a small, black Russian-made Lada. Mikhail drives, and David and Jaanika sit in the backseats.

"This looks like a KGB car from long ago," David quips. "I hope it runs better than the Soviet variety."

"Don't worry. I installed a new engine," Mikhail says.

Mikhail starts to drive through Minsk's streets. The car enters the main highway and travels in the direction of the Russia–Belarus border.

The Lada travels through Borisov, Platsk, and Navapolatsk on its way to the Russian border. Outside

Novapolask, David notices a blue and green Toyota following his car and recognizes it as a Belarus police car. The police car continues to follow several car lengths behind the Lada. After ten minutes, the light on top of the car begins to flash, and a siren sounds loudly.

"I think the police are on to us. We must have been under the hood," Mikhail warns.

Mikhail presses on the accelerator of the Lada, which rapidly increases the car's speed. The Lada begins to accelerate as the roar of the engine becomes loud. The car weaves erratically through traffic in an attempt to lose the police car following it. The police car attempts to follow the Lada as it changes lanes.

"I think this situation calls for evasive action," David announces. David leans out of the car's window. He takes his pistol out, takes aim at the front of the car, and begins firing rapidly. The pops from the gunshots echo within the car. The smell of smoke and gunpowder is ever present. David is sweating as he continues to shoot in a desperate attempt to stop the police.

The Lada passes by a road sign, which states that it's ten kilometers to the Russia–Belarus border. David leans back into the car after all his ammunition is expended.

"Mikhail, how is everything going? We must be close to the Russian border," David asks. He seems quite worried.

"I am not sure how long this engine can take this speed," Mikhail reports worryingly, and he holds the steering wheel as firmly as he can, despite the fact that it's vibrating violently. The loud roar and backfiring of the engine protesting the car's excessive speed can be heard inside the car.

There are two men inside the police car following the Lada. One officer opens the window outside the passenger side of the vehicle. He aims his pistol and fires continuously at the Lada.

The pinging sounds of bullets penetrating the Lada can be heard inside the car. One bullet hits the window and cracks the glass. Jaanika seems quite frightened by this development.

David's expression reveals he is quite angry. He reloads his gun, aims again at the vehicle, and recognizes that the police car is damaged by his gunfire, as bullet holes appear to have pierced the front windshield. The pops of David's gun ring out as he continues to expend the ammunition within his pistol.

The sounds of sirens amplify as two other Belarus police cars join the chase behind the car. A policeman continues firing at the Lada from the passenger side of the vehicle.

A bullet penetrates the side window of the Lada. "They are getting closer! There are too many of them!" David yells to Mikhail.

The Lada moves from the middle lane to the right lane. "Holy shit!" Mikhail yells. He spots a roadblock up ahead and sees that his car is fast approaching the trap.

"Mikhail, we need to do something fast!" Jaanika warns.

"Don't worry. The Belarus police don't know how to improvise. I know a route off the main road. This will take them by surprise!" Mikhail yells. He takes a sharp right turn, heads off the main highway, and travels on a small dirt road, which follows a forested tract of land.

The bumps of the road are apparent inside the Lada; Jaanika and David are rocked from side to side as the car travels at an accelerated pace and is steered erratically. The sirens of the police cars can be heard blaring in the distance. David appears nervously sweating.

The speedometer increases to 100 miles an hour. The car begins to shudder.

"I am not sure this car is meant to go this fast," David states and looks worriedly at Jaanika.

"*Joo!*" Jaanika remarks.

The Lada drives over an outcropped tree stump. The front tire and then undercarriage of the car are launched upward at great speed into the air. Jaanika lowers her head, anticipating the worst. David appears startled, and his eyes open wide in horror. Mikhail attempts to control the car by turning the steering wheel to the left. After several seconds in the air, the Lada drops back to the ground like a brick in flight. It lands on the right tire and tilts right. It rolls over on its side, and the body of the vehicle skids on the ground for several seconds, making an awful grinding sound within the car.

David is thrown from the car and lands in a nearby ditch. David observes the car coming to a violent stop several yards away. All is silent in the woods. David brushes himself off. He slowly rises from the ground and walks in the direction of the damaged vehicle. David approaches the car. The Lada appears to be severely damaged. David acts quickly. He uses all his strength and wrestles the dented back door open. He looks inside and is relieved to find Jaanika still alive.

"Are you injured?" David asks. David appears very concerned.

"None the worse for wear, considering the situation," Jaanika remarks. She is stuck in the backseat.

David takes Jaanika's hand and assists her in getting out of the vehicle. Jaanika sits down next to the car for a moment and checks her hair for any blood. David opens the front door of the car and examines Mikhail. He appears to be unresponsive.

"I think Mikhail is dead," David says. He sighs. He checks Mikhail's pulse and does not feel any response.

Jaanika begins to sob. The sirens of the police cars can be heard rapidly approaching in the distance. David spots a marker several yards away. It has the symbol of "The Russian Federation."

"Let's head to Russia. We have little time, as the police will be here very soon," David remarks.

"I wish we could take Mikhail with us," Jaanika remarks distraught.

"I don't think there is anything we can do to help Mikhail," David remarks solemnly.

Both David and Jaanika walk past the border marker and into Russia and an uncertain future.

Chapter 28

Escape to Estonia

The death of Mikhail lays heavy on the minds of David and Jaanika as they travel on a train rapidly heading in the direction of the Russian northwestern border town of Pskov. Jaanika is quiet and appears solemn as she sits beside David.

"We are not dead yet!" David smiles and puts his arm around Jaanika's shoulder in an attempt to comfort her.

"I wish there was something I could have done for Mikhail," Jaanika whispers. She looks despondent and sullen.

"You can save many more people if we can reach Finland. I hope that will make you feel a little happier," David advises.

"I need to tell you something," Jaanika whispers. She takes out a pen, writes on several pieces of paper, and surreptitiously hands them to David. David takes the pieces of paper in hand. They read: *I work for the KaPo, the Kaisepolitsei, in Estonia, which is Estonia's secret police. I have been trained for operational intelligence activities. I have obtained documents that are key to Russia's plan for an invasion of Finland from a source inside the Belarus military intelligence. It seems that Russian and paramilitary forces will attempt to occupy the Aland Islands and the southern Finnish–Russian border. All the electronic documents were inserted into my arm in a chip. Give this to the SUPO or the Finnish government.* Jaanika places a thumb drive into David's hand. David gives back the papers back to Jaanika, and she rips them up. David is a little startled by this news.

"I don't think I am meant to be doing this. I care too much about people. I was just born hearing about Estonia, a mythical land, and wanted to help out the country in its time of need. The Russians are quite aggressive now," Jaanika says. She appears quite despondent.

"Perhaps, you can use your talents in other avenues. I would worry about your future career later. We have to survive to live another day. I would concentrate on that," David warns.

The train halts with a loud screech. The conductor announces in Russian, "Welcome to Pskov."

All the passengers on the train exit the carriage. David turns on his cell phone. He discovers he has received a text message. David reads it. It states: *At 2 p.m., meet me at the hotel in downtown Pskov. Ivan.*

David walks off the train into Pskov's central train station. "Jaanika, we have to head to the hotel for a meeting with our contact, who will assist us in leaving Russia. He worked at the United States embassy in Helsinki for a while, so I trust him." Both Jaanika and David walk into downtown Pskov and observe the beautiful orthodox churches that dominate the landscape. They spot a small boutique and walk inside looking for clothes for Jaanika.

David looks at all the women's clothes and then peers at Jaanika. An idea seems to be germinating within his mind. "Buy something stylish and less Belarus KGB-like." David hands her ten thousand rubles. Jaanika picks out a traditional peasant dress and goes to a small booth in the back of the store, where she changes. She then walks out of the changing room and shows her new look to David as if she was in a fashion show.

"You look beautiful and more like the young girl I remember in Minnesota," David says. He smiles warmly.

"Good. I like the peasant girl look. The KGB look is way too Soviet-retro for me," Jaanika retorts. She twirls around, showing off her new outfit to David.

"Let's head to the hotel," David says.

Jaanika and David hail a taxi. The taxi stops. Jaanika and David get inside. "Take me to Sokos Hotel," David states in Russian.

The driver quickly transports them through the streets of central Pskov. The Pskov fortress and White Holy Trinity Church loom over the city. After several minutes, they arrive at the hotel and exit the cab.

"Let's buy some coffee. We will meet our contact soon," David remarks. David and Jaanika sit at the table for a while. Both seem a little tense and quiet. David scans the area for any signs of surveillance by the Russian Federal Security Service.

"I wish I could contact my family," Jaanika states and appears unhappy and sullen.

"We are on the run. When we get back, this will be possible. I promise you, Jaanika," David remarks.

A six foot two–inch man wearing jeans and a black coat approaches the table. "I am Ivan. Please come with me, and we will brief you about the trip over the border."

Jaanika and David get up from the table and walk to a room that is located at a nearby hotel. David is shocked when he enters the hotel room, when he sees several men wearing green military uniforms. They raise their weapons and aim them at Jaanika and David.

"You are being detained!" one armed man wearing fatigues remarks.

David appears quite angry.

Cliff Armstrong saunters into the room. He sits down. David looks quite confused.

"David, welcome to Russia." Cliff smiles.

"Cliff, who are these people? Russian Federal Security Service Officers?" David questions.

"No, they are part of the Siloviki group that you know well. They are employed at the United States embassy as the Embassy Surveillance and Security Team," Cliff says.

"What are you doing in Russia?" David asks puzzled. David looks around the room.

"I am here to prevent you from delivering information to the Finns, Estonians, or the Americans. I warned you that I would kill you if I found out that you were CIA. You can't only be working for the Department of State. When the SUPO detained you, I suspected you were more than a Consular Affairs employee," Cliff says.

"Cliff, why would you want to prevent us from returning to Finland? We don't have any intelligence. I think you are delusional at this point," David questions. David tries to play the game. A bluff is always a good option.

"Listen, this is a new era. America is in decline. Some of Finland's resources have been promised to me if I cooperate," Cliff retorts. He sits back in his chair and points with his right hand at David.

"I thought you said you believed in America?" David asks. He appears to be quite angry.

"Sure, it's the land of financial opportunity. However, my opportunity is clearly with the Russians at this moment. Russia is rising now. *Rossiya vozvrashchayetsya k svoyemu utrachennomu velichiyu!* David, you should remember this. Russia is no longer the weak country of the 1990s or early 2000s," Cliff quips. "You are Russian by birth. It's your country, too. Your future is with Russia, too," Cliff says.

David is quiet for a moment. "Cliff, Russia is where I was born. Russia's return to greatness has nothing to do with me. My loyalty should not be questioned. I work for the United States government and spent most of my life in New York City, after all," David remarks.

Cliff chuckles a little. "You should know that the CIA tried to kill you when you first arrived in Finland. That is how they repaid your loyalty. You're either dumb or very naive."

"What are you talking about?" David remarks. David looks a little confused.

"This is the age of global commerce. You should take advantage of all the opportunities offered to you. Why should you be the exception?" Cliff lectures.

"How do you know all this?" David inquires.

"The Department of State headquarters ordered me to stop our internal investigation of the death of your wife when we got too close to the truth," Cliff remarks. He sits down and pauses. "I'm sorry to say that you and your Estonian friend will have to be liquidated. We can't let Finns know the plans for the Russian takeover, and I am not going to torture you for the information," Cliff says.

"It seems like you bought the United States ambassadorship to Finland and now the Russians have purchased your loyalty," David remarks angrily.

Cliff nonverbally orders the men to take Jaanika and David out of the room. The men raise their guns and point them at David and Jaanika as they walk them out of the room. With guns pointed to their backs,

David and Jaanika are directed to enter the backseat of a black Russian-made car. The driver travels from central Pskov to a wooded area located outside the city. The car stops. David and Jaanika sit within the car with guns pointed at their backs. The car stops. The men motion for both of them to exit the car.

The men push David and Jaanika as they walk into the center of an open field. The two point, indicating for Jaanika and David to stand still. One man gives a nonverbal signal to several men standing twenty yards away. The two gunmen aim their weapons in preparation to shoot.

"Jaanika, I am sorry I failed. I wish things did not have to end this way," David remarks. David looks worried. He glances at the Nordic cross he is wearing.

"No worries," Jaanika says. She shakes with fear.

Loud sounds of gunfire ring out in the distance. A man with a gun aimed at David falls down and appears dead. David is astonished by this development. Another shot rings out, and another man drops. Another gunman standing to the side of David and Jaanika panics and begins to run away. Another sound of a gunshot rings out loudly, and a bullet penetrates his brain. He falls to the ground and is motionless.

"Let's go!" David shouts. He seizes the moment and takes Jaanika by the hand. They both run and take cover behind a huge spruce tree.

A black jeep rapidly drives up. A female and two men exit the car. All are carrying automatic weapons. David recognizes Pia and several other SUPO agents.

"*Terve!*" Pia announces. She smiles.

"I have never been so happy to see you. How did you find us?" David asks. He sports a huge smile.

"I put a tracking device in the Nordic cross I gave you in the sauna," Pia says. Pia walks with David and Jaanika over to the car. "We have to head out of Russia as soon as possible. The FSB and Russian authorities will know something is up soon, and they are now searching for Jaanika. I think Ambassador Armstrong tipped them off about her," Pia warns.

David and Jaanika open the car door. David gets in the front seat and drives the car. The car accelerates and drives out of the countryside, heading in the direction of the Russian–Estonian border. Pia is also sitting in the front seat beside David.

The car drives out of the dirt road in the woods and onto a small highway.

"We are only about two miles from the Estonian border. The sooner we get out of Russia, the better," Pia remarks.

"I am hoping for no problems before we get to the border. This day has been too event-filled for me," David quips.

"*Joo,*" Jaanika says while sitting in the backseat.

David spots a roadblock of two Russian police cars in the distance; they are blocking the road and appear to be conducting searches of all cars passing through the road.

"I spoke too soon." David abruptly turns the steering wheel to the right and maneuvers the car to the side of the road. The vehicle veers off the paved road and travels in a heavily forested area along a dirt road that follows the main road. The car is jolted by the bumps in the road. David swerves the vehicle to avoid hitting trees, bushes, and rocks. A great whirling sound is heard from above. Several people in the car look up to the sky to spot the drone. "I think the Russian border guards have spotted us. There is an unmanned vehicle flying overhead," Jaanika remarks.

A loud bang and a thud ensue. The explosion can be heard coming from behind the car.

"What the hell was that?" David yells.

"We are under fire," Pia remarks. She looks quite concerned.

The car continues to accelerate as the speedometer reaches ninety miles an hour. Moments later, a large black elk appears from nowhere and runs out in front of the car. David turns the steering wheel, and the screeching and whirl of the tires sound loudly as they make an evasive maneuver. The elk strikes the car and bounces off the hood with a large thud. The impact of the collision causes the jeep to spin out of control, skidding in circles. It quickly comes to a stop as the motor quits.

David is shell-shocked by the accident. He looks in the back of the car. "Hope everyone is OK. We should have only a few hundred meters to the border. We will have to do it on foot. It should be easier to cross the Russian–Estonian border in this area. It's heavily forested. Hopefully, there is less security in this sector," David says.

Pia, Jaanika, David, and the two SUPO agents exit the jeep. They begin to trudge through the forestland. They see a spy drone that continues to fly overhead. David spots a border marker in the distance. It states, "*Essti*", which means Estonia. He appears quite relieved.

"Halt!" Several solders with blue and white flags on their uniforms aim their weapons at David, Pia, and Jaanika.

David places his hands up.

"We are friends," Jaanika yells in Estonian. She flashes a friendly and relieved smile.

The men begin to smile, too. "Who are you?" they remark in Estonian.

"I am Jaanika Olson. I work with the Estonian government. The KaPo. We are here to provide you valuable information. We need to head to Tallinn as soon as possible. Is it possible to use your vehicle?" Jaanika asks.

"I can give you a lift if you want. I just have to check with my chain of command first. I need to confirm your identity, too," the border guard mentions. The guard talks on the radio for several minutes. He walks them to the border post. They wait.

The Estonia border guard approaches Jaanika after several minutes. "We can head to Tallinn. I have received orders to take you there immediately," the Estonian border guard mentions.

David, Jaanika, and Pia enter an Estonian military jeep, which drives on the highway, rapidly heading in the direction of Tallinn.

David looks at Jaanika. "You will be able to talk with your family soon. You should smile a little. I need some Minnesota nice right now."

Jaanika flashes a smile.

David is alarmed by the sound of gunshots, which land with a thud as they penetrate the interior of the car. He is confused.

"Do you hear those gunshots, too?" David asks the border guard who is sitting in the driver's seat.

"I heard them, but I am not sure where they are coming from," he remarks.

Pia and David pull their weapons out and scan the area, looking for the source of the gunfire. David looks around and spots a black BMW following them. It appears that the driver is shooting from the front seat of the car.

David takes out his pistol, aims at the BMW, and begins to fire several rounds of ammunition in the direction of the car.

"Take my gun!" the soldier urges and hands it to David.

"I will call for backup," the border guard yells. He contacts the Estonian military on his wireless radio.

"Thanks. I need a real weapon. This has nice firepower," David retorts.

David picks up the Uzi submachine gun. He sprays a volley of bullets at the car; they penetrate the car and mark it with holes in the front window and the driver's side. The occupant of the BMW continues to fire at David's car.

"I am hit!" Jaanika yelps.

David stops shooting and reaches in the back of the car in an attempt aid Jaanika. "Let me look at your wound." David inspects the area where Jaanika is hit. Jaanika's shoulder appears to have been grazed by a bullet.

"How do you feel?" David asks. He looks concerned.

"I will survive. We have to complete this mission and deliver the plans to the KaPo," Jaanika retorts, grimacing in pain as she touches her shoulder.

David picks up his Uzi and lets out several bursts of gunfire. The rat-a-tat-tat of the burst of rounds firing echo inside the car and strike the BMW's front window. Moments later, it rolls off the road and crashes into a tree on the side of the median

David's jeep stops abruptly, and everyone in the car gets out and attempts to identify the occupant of the BMW. David follows the Estonia border guard with his pistol in hand. He manages to open the door and looks inside to identify the occupant. He looks at the badly injured body and discovers it's Cliff Armstrong.

"I will call the ambulance. He appears critically injured," the Estonian border remarks.

"We have to get to KaPo headquarters as soon as possible," David states.

David, Jaanika, Pia, and the SUPO officers enter the jeep and again speed rapidly in the direction of Tallinn.

Several Russian Bear aircraft can be viewed flying overhead on a possible reconnaissance mission, as Jaanika, Pia, and David enter the outskirts of Tallinn. At 7:00 p.m., they all arrive at KaPo headquarters. David, Pia, Jaanika get out of the car and enter the KaPo headquarters.

A man in a suit and tie approaches Jaanika. "Where are the plans?" he inquires in Estonian.

"I had a chip inserted into my arm with the Russian attack plans on them. You need to extract the chip as soon as possible," she remarks.

The man escorts Jaanika out of the room. Pia looks at David. "We need to get back to Finland. Let's take an Estonian military helicopter from Tallinn to Helsinki. I was briefed before I left that the latest intelligence indicates that Russia may launch an attack at any time," Pia remarks.

"Let's go," David remarks.

Chapter 29

Federal Security Service Crackdown in Karelia

Close to the Russian–Finnish border in the formerly Finnish-controlled Karelian capital of Petrozavodsk, thousands of protestors stand behind barricades next to the Karelian governor's headquarters and the region's administrative offices. Each is clapping to signal their protest of the Russian government authorities' imprisonment of the once democratically elected governor and member of the Finn League. The protestors carry placards stating, "Free the imprisoned opposition." They shout "Freedom for Karelia." Opposite the protestors stand hundreds of men in dark police uniforms with police insignia. They carry batons, helmets, and shields. These are the tools of the Russian elite OMON police.

The police officers appear to have received their orders, as each man readies his riot gear and stands at attention. The riot policemen begin to march in formation in the direction of the protestors. They throw tear gas at the protestors, and the gas whirls in the air and lands within the mass of demonstrators protesting in the square. Protestors respond by fleeing in the opposite direction to avoid the effects of the tear gas. A man wearing a dark coat approaches, picks up a fuming tear-gas canister, and immediately throws it in the air. It whirls in an upward arch and lands in the vicinity of the riot police who threw it.

Hundreds of OMON forces with wooden batons approach the protestors in formation and start to beat and handcuff, young men, old ladies, and women. The OMON troops take down the Finnish and Karelian flags and destroy them. Chaos seems to ensue. Men and women are seen running chaotically. The bloodied faces of OMON victims quickly appear throughout the crowd. Several protestors appear enraged, while others sit in the square crying solemnly.

"Disperse! This protest has become too large. You are violating your permit. You will be arrested," a member of the OMON announces on the loudspeaker that echoes throughout the plaza.

Several protestors begin to hurl back stones in the direction of the OMON. One by one, riot policemen and plainclothes officers grab the demonstrators, journalists, and anyone who happens to be watching the event. They beat each person with their batons, handcuff them, and drag them over to an awaiting black van, which will take them to prison.

A battle with police ensues. Loud pops can be heard in the distance. Protestors start falling to the ground. Some can be seen lying in pools of blood. Other protestors flee the scene screaming.

Russians dressed in the traditional nationalistic Cossack dress of long black coats, black vests, and hats, with the emblem of Cossack nationalism, appear in the distance and march in formation over the dead bodies of the protestors. "Death to the traitors! Long live Russia!" they chant and desecrate the bodies lying on the ground.

Lappeenranta/Russian border Crossing

At the Finnish border checkpoint of Valimaa, refugees line the highway as far as the eye can see. All are waiting for a chance to enter Finland and safety from the violence inside Karelia. The loud booms of gunfire echo in the distance. Some shells land on the numerous families sitting in line in their cars waiting to cross the border. Men, women, and children get out of their cars and flee into ditches as they seek cover from the incoming fire from Russian military aircraft.

A Finnish border guard picks up his radio communication device. "We need to know the correct manner to proceed. Refugees want to cross. We are experiencing gunfire but don't know where the gunfire is originating. It may be the Russian military or paramilitary forces. I await your orders."

Chapter 30

The Ambush

The whistles and static of the shortwave radio blare loudly within the small Helsinki apartment. A woman's voice announcing coded numbers in Russian can be barely heard within the static and interference of the broadcast. Mikhailovich meticulously writes down every number onto the paper lying before him. He decodes the information with a key he has taken out of his pocket. He looks at the message he has received from KGB headquarters. It reads, *Prime Minister Tarja Manninen primary target. CIA Chief, Kallio, Helsinki, Finland second target.*

A chill goes down Mikhailovich's spine as the significance of his orders become apparent. He has to make a critical decision. Mikhailovich isn't happy with the news of the target selection, but he is a soldier. He is determined to carry out a successful operation for the survival of his family in Belarus.

"Have you received the names of the targets from Minsk yet?" Vladimir questions. He paces around the apartment appearing quite nervous.

"Yes, we have our targets identified. Pack up the weapons and prepare for an operation. You should know the operational procedures," Mikhailovich orders. He picks up the deciphered message, lights a match, and proceeds to burn the paper in the kitchen sink; this will hide all evidence of the mission.

"Yes, sir." Vladimir looks excited. With military precision, he assembles all the equipment in order. He is ready to commence the operation.

Both Vladimir and Mikhailovich exit the apartment after having destroyed any record of their stay in the small safe house. Each carries a green knapsack as they board the tram. They are both standing in the tram and appear quiet as they travel.

"We are going to a hotel near the Finnish parliament and will carry out the operation," Mikhailovich whispers and glances at Vladimir, who is now sitting in the tram.

After fifteen minutes, they exit the tram at the city center and begin to walk to a small hotel, which is located near the parliament.

Mikhailovich walks into the hotel and approaches the front desk. "I need a place to stay for a couple of days," he remarks.

"We will need your passports," the hotel desk attendant says. She presents a friendly smile.

"Sure," Mikhailovich says. He hands the woman two Estonian passports. One possesses the name Dmitry Ivanovich and the other Juhani Holm.

"Welcome to Helsinki," the Finnish hotel attendant says and hands Mikhailovich the keys to the hotel room.

"Thanks," Mikhailovich remarks.

Ivan and Mikhailovich walk up to the third floor of the hotel and set down their equipment on the table located next to the television.

Mikhailovich turns on the television to provide background noise. He approaches the hotel room's window to see if there are any signs of surveillance. He appears a little apprehensive.

Mikhailovich sits down at the small table in the apartment. He motions for Vladimir to sit next to him in an empty chair.

"Here is the brief for our mission. We have finally received all our orders from Minsk and the intelligence to support the mission. The prime minister of Finland is our prime target. We know that she jogs once a day early in the morning outside her office before she starts work. Her bodyguard may jog with her. This will be our opportunity to take her out. We will then target the CIA chief in Helsinki. This will be just revenge for the provocation Finland caused by violating our airspace. We must be methodical and precise. I don't need to tell you that this is a very dangerous mission, and all procedures have to be followed to make it a success," Mikhailovich whispers.

"Yes, sir. What weapon should we use?" Vladimir inquires. He appears quite excited. He takes out his weapon and fiddles with his revolver as he sits at the table.

"Success for this mission will require excellent long-range shooting abilities to take out the Finnish prime minister. I am sure you are up to it," Mikhailovich says. He smiles a little and remarks, "This is only our first target. You will have lots of chances to use your operational tradecraft. Let's get some rest. We will make an attempt tomorrow. This is for the honor of Belarus!"

At 3:00 a.m., Mikhailovich and Vladimir awake to the sound of the alarm clock. They check out of the hotel and walk several blocks to a park located few blocks from the Finnish parliament, which sits next to the Baltic Sea.

There are several bushes located a hundred yards from the path, which runs through the center of Helsinki. Mikhailovich decides to set up his operation there. He takes his rifle out of the knapsack, assembles it, and loads the ammunition. He also takes out small binoculars. Vladimir possesses a pistol and a rifle with a scope.

Mikhailovich spots several runners. He looks through the viewfinder of the rifle but does not recognize any of the runners as being the prime minister. He lowers his weapon and waits impatiently in the bushes.

At 4:40 a.m., an entourage of joggers runs along the path. There are five people jogging in the group. He feels the adrenaline rush through his veins. He attempts to concentrate. He looks through his binoculars and recognizes the prime minister running with several other people who are following her in a pack. He spots several security personnel in her detail. She is wearing a blue and white jogging suit.

"That must be her," Mikhailovich whispers. He picks up the rifle lying next to him. He looks through the site finder and spots the prime minister running. Mikhailovich pulls the trigger. The click of the trigger echoes within Mikhailovich's ears. To his horror, nothing happens. He attempts to pull the trigger again, and nothing happens again. The gun appears to have jammed.

"Shit!" Mikhailovich yells.

Vladimir looks at Mikhailovich puzzled. He takes out his weapon in an attempt to aim at the prime minister. He reaches for the trigger.

"No!" Mikhailovich says. He takes the gun in Vladimir's hand and wrestles it from Vladimir.

"What's wrong?" Vladimir questions. He appears confused.

"We will have another chance. We missed our window of opportunity for today. The prime minister just got lucky this time. I think God is on her side, as the rifle should have fired. I tested it before the mission. We will concentrate on the second target and then take her out next. The CIA target should be an easy operation," Mikhailovich says.

"Yes, sir," Vladimir says. He looks a little stunned.

The prime minister can be seen continuing to run in the distance. The two men pack their equipment in knapsacks and travel over to David's residence, which is located in the Kallio District of Helsinki.

"Let's head into the building across from the target location. It appears to be a hotel," Mikhailovich orders. He walks down the street.

"Yes, sir!" Vladimir responds.

Mikhailovich walks up to the hotel's front office. "We would like to stay for two nights. We would like a sixth-floor apartment. Do you have one with a street view?" he asks.

The hotel clerk checks her computer system. "You are very lucky. Summer is the high season here. We have a small room available. Will that be OK?" the clerk inquires.

"Yes," Mikhailovich responds.

"We need to hold your passport and those of all your guests," the clerk, who is standing at the front desk, informs him.

Mikhailovich presents two Polish passports to the clerk.

"Thank you, Mr. Novak," the clerk remarks and hands the keys to Mikhailovich.

Both Mikhailovich and Vladimir enter the apartment and open the window facing the street. Mikhailovich looks out the window and can see that David's apartment window can be clearly viewed from their vantage point.

"We will stay here to observe our target. You will report any activity to me," Mikhailovich orders.

"Yes, sir," Vladimir responds.

After a day of observing no activity inside the apartment, Mikhailovich sits in the apartment and has become nervous. He has sent several messages about meeting with David but has not received any response. "It appears that David is not home. I think we need to case his apartment, set up some devices, and be ready for when he returns," Mikhailovich orders

"Yes, sir," Vladimir says.

Vladimir proceeds to take several cameras and other equipment for the operation and places them inside his backpack. He puts on the backpack and exits the hotel room.

He walks down the stairs and across the street. He observes several individuals entering and exiting the apartment and is able to enter easily using the excuse of having lost a key to gain entry.

Vladimir walks into the apartment complex, walks up the stairs, and approaches David's apartment door. He hesitates for moment. He looks left and right and does not see anyone in the hallways. He quickly sticks a pick into the lock and unhinges the bottom lock. He disables the top lock quickly and enters David's apartment. He walks into the dark corridors of the apartment and begins to insert a listening device in the living room wall. He walks to David's room and installs another bug.

A man, who is wearing a hood and ski mask, silently enters David's apartment. He holds a gun in his hand. He slowly walks inside and looks around. He hears activity in David's bedroom. He slowly approaches and sees Vladimir busily at work inside the bedroom.

The man spots Vladimir within the sights of his gun. He quickly fires several rounds with his silencer. The pings of the bullets can be heard in the apartment. Vladimir is hit in the chest and the head and falls to the floor. He appears to be dead.

The masked man walks out of the apartment undetected.

Mikhailovich sits in the room with the Russian-language Finnish TV channel blaring as he continues to watch David's apartment. The announcer states, "The Belarus president has announced the country's incorporation into Russia again. The Belarus security-based KGB is now unleashing a wave of repression not seen since the Stalin purges."

Mikhailovich feels the chill of deep-seated fear. He wonders, *Will my protector be purged? Are my family members now in danger? Will jail await me upon my return to Belarus?*

A masked man slowly approaches Mikhailovich from behind. He raises his hand and hits him over the head with the butt of his gun. Mikhailovich falls to the floor and is knocked unconscious.

Chapter 31

The Assassin

David and Pia approach an awaiting Finnish military helicopter at Tallinn's heliport. The helicopter blades rotating emits a loud roar. David opens the door of the aircraft. Pia and David enter the passenger seats and fasten their seat belts in preparation for the short journey to Helsinki. The helicopter pilot, who is sitting upfront, gives the nonverbal signal for David and Pia to prepare for takeoff. The aircraft quickly rises in the air, leaves Tallinn's harbor, and rapidly flies over the Baltic Sea toward Helsinki, Finland.

David takes out his smartphone and checks his government email. He notices a new email titled, *Belarus Department of State Country Update, National Emergency Declared. Dateline Minsk, Belarus.*

David opens the email and eagerly reads the content. It states, *Belarus' President Lukashenko has declared a national emergency and has announced that Belarus will be temporarily absorbed into Russian in view of the threats from NATO. In response to this announcement, KGB officials announced the suspension of all civil liberties. All political activities have been suspended, and protests are now banned. Reports have been filtering in of mass arrests of perceived opponents and wholesale Stalin-like purges being conducted of the Belarus military, civil service, and anyone they perceive as being against this new policy.*

Pia looks at David solemnly. "I have some news for you."

"What is it?" David questions.

"I think the CIA is searching for you, as the United States embassy has informed the Finnish Police that they want to be alerted if we encounter you," Pia says.

"Did you inform them of my activities and current location?" David asks. David appears concerned. Evading the CIA was not a part of his plan.

"I told them I had not seen you. I am not sure how long I can continue to lie to the CIA and the United States Department of State," Pia remarks. She looks quite worried. "I know of information that will also be of interest to you. We matched the prints on one of the guns we recently uncovered at your summer home. The prints are a positive match to a motorcycle gang member's fingerprints we have on file. He is located in Helsinki. He is a United States and Finnish citizen named Jose Lopez," Pia says.

A chill goes down David's spine. He glances at Pia. "Are you going to arrest Lopez?"

"We are looking for him at the moment. He seems to have gone underground. He is suspected of having worked as a professional hit man and drug runner. However, we never had enough evidence to charge him. Finland's National Directorate of Investigation is investigating the murder," Pia says. Pia glances momentarily at her smartphone to see all incoming emails.

The helicopter continues its rapid journey over the Baltic Sea. The choppy waters of the Baltic Sea are evident from above. David peers down for a moment and sees huge ferries traveling to Swedish, Russian, and Baltic ports.

David looks at Pia. He decides it's the proper time to break the news to her. "My excursion to Belarus may have paid off for you with good intelligence. It appears that Russia will use the unrest in Karelia to start an occupation of Finnish territory on its eastern Russian border and also occupy Aland in the Baltic Sea. They plan to use unconventional forces to take over several border checkpoints and the Finnish town of Lappeenranta. The objective is to force a change in Finnish foreign policy that is pro-Russia from its current pro-EU stance," David informs.

"This would be of great interest," Pia states. She furiously types an email to SUPO headquarters on her smartphone.

"Here is a thumb drive with the Belarus and Russian military documents. I have some personal business to attend to," David mentions. He hands the thumb drive to Pia.

"You can't just leave after providing me with the intelligence. I will have many questions for you," Pia says. She looks serious.

"I have a mission to complete. I hope you understand," David says.

The helicopter approaches Finland. The small islands outside of Helsinki come into view. Helsinki Harbor, with its giant ferries parked adjacent to the central marketplace, can be viewed below. The military helicopter soon touches down outside Helsinki.

Pia looks at David. "What are you going to do now?" Pia asks.

"I need time to consider my options. I am playing a very dangerous game at this point. I am aware that many people want me dead now," David says.

"If you need any assistance, let me know. Please call me as soon as you can." Pia flashes a friendly smile and hands David her business card.

He proceeds to leave the military base and takes a tram back to his apartment in Kallio. He walks up to his apartment building's main entrance, opens the door, and climbs several flights of stairs. He arrives at his apartment and finds the door unlocked. David looks extremely nervous. He fears that the CIA may be planning to kidnap him or that Russian intelligence may kill him.

He pulls out his pistol from his jacket, slowly opens his door, and enters his darkened apartment with his gun drawn. He slowly walks inside. Immediately, an awful smell hits his face. He grabs a napkin lying on a desk and places it next to his nose to blunt the smell. He peers around in the pitch blackness of his apartment. He sees that all his papers on his desk are a mess. He slowly searches his apartment. He walks into his kitchen and discovers his cabinets are all open and the dishes have been strewn all over the floor. David slowly walks into his bedroom. His gun is drawn, and his senses are heightened to detect and respond to the slightest movement.

David enters his bedroom and discovers the source of the awful smell. He is in shock. On the floor lies the body of a young, Slavic-looking man. The man appears to be about five feet, ten inches tall. He is wearing jeans and a jacket. David approaches the body. The deceased man looks pale and cold. He appears to have been lying there for several days. David reaches into the dead man's pocket and finds a Belarus military ID card. David attempts to read it in the darkness and is able to make out on the card "Vladimir Serkin." It's written in Russian Cyrillic letters.

David recalls that Serkin was the name of one of the Belarus operatives who was located in Helsinki. He is perplexed as to how or why the dead man entered his apartment. Fearing arrest, David decides not to call the police. David takes out his cell phone, writes a message, and sends it to Pia: *There is something in my apartment that you might want to look at. Send some people over to investigate. David.* He sends the message.

David looks under his bed and opens his safe. He takes out all his identity documents and bundles of cash and places them into his backpack. He quickly exits the apartment, walking out the building from the back exit to avoid detection.

David's smartphone buzzes. He looks at it and sees an encrypted text. David opens it. *Let's meet. I have a prize for you. Only contact me this way in the future. Beware of surveillance. Lots of heat now! Lopez.*

David receives a phone call. He knows he only gave out his phone number to one person—Jaanika. He answers it. "Hey, this is Jaanika. I'm back in Helsinki. I am calling as I never got to thank you for helping me out."

"Don't think anything of it. You're family after all, and that is what I think family should do for each other. By the way, how are you feeling?" David asks.

"I am in good shape and recovering from the ordeal," Jaanika says. She touches her shoulder and winces a little in pain.

"Where are you now? I am in Helsinki now and am located near my apartment in Kallio," Jaanika states.

"I'm located close to you. Can we meet for a couple of minutes?" David inquires.

"I am at the *Musta Kissa* bar in Kallio. It's the place that all the Kallio bohemians frequent. Do you know where that is located?" Jaanika states.

"Sure. I may not be a hipster, but I know a good place to enjoy a coffee. I will be over there shortly."

David walks down the street for several blocks. He scans the area to see if he is being followed. He arrives at the bar where Jaanika is located. He looks around and sees Jaanika sitting at a table with a beer in hand. She is wearing blue jeans and a red sweater. He notices that Jaanika's shoulder is bandaged.

David walks up behind her. "*Terve*, Jaanika. How are you?"

"I am good considering all that has happened to me. I talked with my family. They thank you for your assistance," Jaanika says.

David proceeds to sit down in a chair located beside Jaanika. "I have a mission I have to go on. I'm not sure I will come back alive. Tell my family I love them if anything happens," David says. He appears worried.

"Where are you going?" Jaanika asks. She looks quite puzzled.

"I can't tell you, but I'm glad you're safe," David remarks.

"I talked to several employees of the United States embassy in Helsinki when I arrived. They asked me where you were located. Should I provide them with the information?" Jaanika asks.

"Thanks for letting me know. Please say you don't know anything about my location in Finland if you are asked again, and don't give out my current cell phone number to anyone. I have issues with the United States government presently," David says.

"Is there anything else I can do to assist you?" Jaanika says. She looks concerned.

"No, I'm just glad you're safe. Jaanika, Can I offer you some advice?" David says. Jaanika nods in approval.

"I want you to know that there is life after working in an intelligence agency. I was employed by the CIA until recently," David states.

Jaanika's expression reveals that she is quite surprised. "What were you doing in the CIA?" Jaanika asks.

"That's for another time," David says. David hugs Jaanika and walks away. He walks to the subway and travels to the eastern section of Helsinki, known as Itäkeskus. He is careful to observe any possible signs of surveillance and sees nothing, to his relief. He arrives at his destination, which is a new immigrant enclave that contains signs in Arabic, Finnish, and Somali hanging from storefronts. David walks out of the subway exit, looks at his smartphone, and observes a new message: *I see you.* It appears to be Lopez texting him.

David looks around and does not see anyone. He is startled as he feels an intense pressure to his back that hurts.

"*Que pasa?* I have a gun, so follow me," Lopez orders. He pushes David forward.

"Nice meeting you again," David retorts. He looks a little angry. He might have trusted Lopez too much.

"Follow me, and nothing will happen to you." David walks with a gun pointed at his back. They both walk down the street.

"Can't we talk about this calmly?" David explains. He continues walking with the gun pointed at his back.

"Make a right turn into the alleyway. I will kill you if I have to, *mi amigo*," Lopez orders.

"You're the boss, I guess," David says. He continues to walk.

"I know I am. Now walk up these stairs and into the apartment complex." Lopez directs David through the back door of a 1960s' Soviet-style apartment building.

Both David and Lopez slowly walk up five flights of stairs.

"David, don't try anything. I need you to open the door to the stairwell and go to room 512," Lopez orders. He sticks his guns deeply into David's back.

"That's painful . . . OK, I get your point. You're in charge. I think we can do business. Killing me will not get you any more money," David remarks.

Lopez opens his apartment door and directs David to walk inside.

David plays coy. He looks back at Lopez. "What is this about? I am preparing for an operation. We have a deal you know." David plays his cards. He is judging what Lopez's next move may be.

"The Finnish police are looking for me. I have to be careful," Lopez retorts. "I am not sure if you're a snitch. I will kill you if I think you are," Lopez says.

Lopez then points his left hand in the direction of a room located at the back of the apartment.

"I have a present for you." Lopez smiles. David walks into the room and sees Ivan Mikhailovich with his hands tied sitting in the corner. His face appears bloodied and bruised.

"I was tracking them and caught him searching for you in your apartment." Lopez laughs. "I'm tougher than the Belarus KGB," he remarks and sports an immense self-satisfied smirk on his face.

"What will you give me for him? He was going to kill you. I just learned this information," Lopez says.

"I thought they were here to kill Katya? That is what you told me before," David asks. He looks puzzled.

"I admit. I was wrong. You know that people lie. Everyone lies. Only the Finns don't realize this. They are too honest," Lopez adds. He places the gun at Mikhailovich's head.

A frightened expression flashes across Mikhailovich's face.

"Ok, let's negotiate," David remarks. He looks around the apartment to see if any other gunmen are present in case the meeting results in bloodshed, and he's relieved to see no one else there.

"I want cash now," Lopez orders. "I saved your ass from death. The CIA must have put up the money for the teddy bear bombing flight to Belarus. They wanted revenge. They wanted to kill the CIA's chief of station. That is you, from what I have heard," Lopez says.

"What do you say about this Mikhailovich?" David questions. He is not sure if Lopez is telling the truth. He knows that Lopez killed his wife and can't be trusted. He also likes to bate Lopez to keep him off guard.

"He is lying. I told you why I am here," Mikhailovich says.

"Don't believe that motherfucker! I want the money now," Lopez states. He brandishes his pistol and appears a little unhinged. He beats Mikhailovich with the pistol with multiple blows to his chest. Mikhailovich recoils in pain.

David remains silent for a moment. His analyst instincts kick into gear again as he assesses whom to believe. This is a matter of life and death.

A huge explosion rocks the apartment to its foundations. The windows shatter. The front door is blown off its hinges. David, Mikhailovich, and Lopez fall to the floor. David attempts to get up from the floor. Men wearing fatigues and possessing weapons rapidly flood the apartment.

"Put your hands up!" several policemen shout forcefully with guns drawn and seemingly ready to shoot due to any act of provocation. It appears to be a Finnish special operations police known as a Karhu team storming the apartment. Lopez looks panicked and quickly draws his gun. He fires several shots at the police. One officer drops to the ground and appears to be injured. Two Finnish policemen return fire from the front of the apartment and aim in Lopez's direction. Lopez is struck in the chest and the throat. He lets out a high-pitch gurgling sound and falls to the floor dead. A pool of blood appears next to his body.

David puts up his hands. Mikhailovich raises his hands also. "I want political asylum!" he yells.

David sees Pia walk in with several other police officers. She approaches David. "Are you OK?"

"I am alright. I am lucky to be alive. Thanks," David says.

"You were playing with fire with Lopez. I warned you. You Americans never listen." Pia pauses for a second. "I liked the intelligence you provided, though."

The SUPO agents enter in plain clothes and escort Mikhailovich out of the apartment in handcuffs.

"Should I be afraid?" David remarks. He looks quite concerned.

Pia smiles. "No. Come with me. There is a person who wants to talk to you." Pia leads the way out of the apartment and into her awaiting car.

Both Pia and David travel to SUPO headquarters. They don't talk in the car. David sits in the car and ponders his next move. He thinks to himself, *Should I negotiate a deal with the SUPO or call the CIA?*

David arrives at SUPO headquarters in Helsinki. Both exit the car, and Pia escorts David through a series of hallways and into a huge office with the SUPO symbol, a lion on top of a sword, prominently displayed on the wall. The SUPO director sits in a seat behind an imposing desk.

"Sit down, David," Jarmo says. He nonverbally directs David toward the chair in front of him. David sits down. Pia quietly leaves the room and shuts the door behind her.

Jarmo looks up from his desk. "Your information has proven to be accurate and actionable intelligence. If you need some help, I can assist you. I know the CIA is not happy with you. You are a wanted person at the moment," Jarmo says.

"Do you know if Lopez killed my wife at the summer home?" David asks. He sits forward and appears quite interested in the answer.

"Yes, it appears he was one of the assassins and had operated with an international gang for hire, which may have connections to US intelligence. We have identified an Iranian and several Serbs working in the group. Lopez also placed a bomb in Bergstrom's car due to a drug-related deal that went bad. We are analyzing the bullets from the dead man in your apartment. It appears that he may have killed him, too. Lopez and the criminal biker gangs now operating in Finland are an American import. Lopez was a freelancer, and he is a new breed of criminal in Finland. I guess I can thank the United States for this development," Jarmo remarks. He looks quite dour.

David appears a little shocked by the news. He tries to keep his composure. "Thank you for your offer of assistance. I need to decide my next move," David remarks.

"Do it quickly. It's tough being a former spy without any cover. I think you have assessed that there may be some retribution directed against you. You have made powerful enemies by leaving the CIA and stealing from the Belarus KGB and the Russian military. You are now caught between two great powers in the multipolar age in which we live. In Finland, we know the feeling well but have survived despite this fact," Jarmo says.

David is quiet for a moment. "Unfortunately, I agree with your assessment. I have become a de-anonymized operative. This is a term of the digital age, which is a corruption of the anonymizer used to mask browsers for those seeking to search the Internet incognito. For me, it means that all my passports have been revoked, my cover has been removed, my credit cards have been suspended, and my name has been placed on every watch list and lookout from Washington DC to Interpol headquarters in Lyon, France. I am an operative who is not out in the cold but who has been exposed to the world in the full light of day. As you know well, this is a very dangerous place to be." David reflects and pauses for a moment. "I am patriot despite what the CIA officials believe. You always make enemies when you do what is right. I will stay in Finland in the meantime. I hope the SUPO will have no objections to my presence in the country," David says.

"You are welcome to stay in Finland. If that changes, I will let you know. The CIA knows you are here, so it may be dangerous to stay," Jarmo says.

"I will take that chance," David says.

"I will wish you the best of luck," Jarmo says.

David shakes Jarmo's hand and walks out of the room and into the streets of Helsinki. The darkness of the rapidly approaching Finland winter is evident from the early sunset. For the first time since his arrival in Finland, David smiles and is at peace, as he knows that Terhi is smiling with him from above.

Chapter 32

Situation Report Karelia/Finnish Border

Helsinki, Finland

Jarmo Bergstrom, the Finnish Security Intelligence Service director, sits in the prime minister's situation room, which is located in Helsinki. Finnish prime minister, Tarja Manninen, and Finnish military defense minister, Timo Holgrum, are also gathered around a long wooden table. A map of the Finnish–Russian border is displayed on a screen stationed in the front of the room.

"We have beefed up our forces along the Finnish–Russian border in Northern Karelia with irregular and conventional troops at key strategic points. The Russians appear to have backed down after we rebuffed their attempts to take over key roads with force in three strategic areas by our new rapid-reaction forces," Timo states. He seems quite subdued.

"Can you tell me what's the situation with the Karelian refugees seeking to enter Finland at the border?" the prime minister inquires as she looks at the briefer outlining the situation.

"We have allowed the refugees to cross from Karelia to Finland. The tide seems to have stemmed at the moment, as the FSB and Russian Guard appear to have stopped their crackdown on perceived Finnish supporters," Timo says.

"Good work in obtaining actionable intelligence about the Russian military. Your information has given us a critical edge defending the border," the Finnish prime minister, Manninen, says. She smiles a little.

"Thank you, Ms. Prime Minister. We have good sources within the SUPO, but in this case, the credit also goes to a bunch of crazy Finns with a small plane, several hundred teddy bears, and a very unusual American," Jarmo remarks.

"*Niin!*" the Finnish prime minister retorts. She smiles.

Chapter 33

A Journey Home

On an early Saturday morning, David wakes up in his temporary home, which is situated in a small cottage in the Finnish countryside. *Life in hiding can be trying on the soul,* David thinks to himself and begins preparations for a perilous journey to Russia to solve the mystery of the disappearance of his wife's remains. Before David begins his journey, he makes sure he possesses his fraudulent Russian passport, a map of Vyborg, and the address of Interex Oy. David knows that his personal mission is dangerous. Both the CIA and Russian intelligence should be searching for him. He walks to his car and changes the license plate from a Finland registration to that of a Russian license plate. He begins a visual inspection of his car for any explosives or tracking devices. After being satisfied that he is safe and nothing is present, David enters the car and starts the ignition. His car's engine roars to life. David presses his foot on the accelerator and proceeds to drive on a dirt road next to the house. He merges onto the main highway and continues to drive east for forty-five minutes. He is tense and apprehensive as he is heading to the Russian border. He spots a sign stating, "20 kilometers to the Finnish–Russian border." David's professional skills kick in and he calms down. As he nears the Russian–Finnish border, David's car slows down behind other cars and waits to cross.

When it's his turn to be inspected, David observes a Russian border guard approaching his car.

"Name," the Russian border guard asks.

"Boris Ivanovich," David says.

"Reason you were visiting Finland?" he questions. He looks at David suspiciously.

"Holiday," David says.

"Did you bring any products banned in Russia from Finland? We have laws against smuggling them into the country," the guard asks.

"Of course not. I'm a Russian patriot. No EU food or products for me." He flashes a fake smile, hoping to seem sincere.

The guard begins an intensive search inside his car. He looks in the backseat and the front seat and nonverbally orders David to open the trunk. David switches the button on his console, and the trunk opens. The guard spends several minutes inspecting the trunk. He then stops searching and completes his inspection. He gives a nonverbal gesture to David to cross into Russia. David places his foot on the accelerator and crosses the border. He drives for thirty minutes. The site of Vyborg, his childhood home, comes into view. He is hit by an emotion he did not expect to feel. Memories of his early childhood and mother and father are awakened within him. He spies a huge white castle, which dominates the town and can be seen prominently from the road. David looks at his map on his cell phone and drives through the center of town and in the direction of an industrial section of Vyborg. He drives past several old, abandoned factories. He parks the car and walks up to a small, dilapidated building, which has several trucks parked at the front. He quickly engages in his normal security precautions to detect surveillance. He approaches the entrance, which has a small broken sign stating "Interex Oy." He walks in through the door and spots an old woman. She looks quite unhappy sitting at her desk.

"*Drasyote*," David remarks.

"*Drasyote*," she responds.

"I was wondering if I might be able to inquire about a shipment of human remains from Lohja to Russia." David sports a friendly smile.

"We don't transport bodies here. Who are you?" the surly woman inquires.

David thinks for a moment. "I'm Boris. I live here in Vyborg. I was inquiring, as I was wondering if you do that sort of thing." David smiles politely.

"Sorry. I can't help you. I am busy at the moment," the woman says.

David walks out of the building. He returns to his car, proceeds to drive for five minutes, and parks the car in a vacant parking lot. He enters the backseat and goes to sleep. David plans to find information in another manner after the company closes its office.

At 9:00 p.m., David wakes up and drives back to Interex Oy. All is dark in the area. David looks around. He approaches the back of the building, which houses the company offices. He takes out his flashlight. He hopes to find a back door or window, which will allow him to search the business. He is surprised at what he sees at the back. It appears that there is a makeshift graveyard. He observes that there are a number of graves that have been dug recently. He also spots a number of coffins stacked on each other. David decides to search the names on all the graves with a flashlight. He walks from gravestone to gravestone, illuminating the name on each grave with the light, searching for the word "Terhi" written on it. David is startled when he hears a Russian voice yell.

"What are you doing? You are trespassing in the graveyard?" a man yells. He appears to be wearing the insignia of a militia officer.

David quickly comes up with a plan. He tries to appear intoxicated. "Sorry, I had to urinate and thought this might be a good area." He flashes a friendly smile.

"What is your name?" the policeman asks.

"Boris," David says. He slurs his words to appear authentic.

"I need to see your ID," the police officer says.

David slowly approaches the officer. His heart is beating rapidly, and his mind is working intensively to dream up a plan. He takes out his passport from his jacket. He gets close to the officer to present his ID, thrusts his fist into the man's face, and knocks him to the ground. He wraps his hand into a fist. He quickly cocks his arm and connects to the man's face and body. He feels possessed. He continues with blow after blow. The man's face appears bloodied and bruised. David gets up from the ground and runs to his car. He is inhaling and exhaling at a fast pace. His nerves are on edge, and adrenaline is rapidly circulating throughout his body. He quickly starts the car's engine and immediately pulls out of the parking lot. He places his foot on the accelerator, and the car speeds up. He continues to drive at a maddening pace on the main highway in the direction of Finland. The roar of the engine overpowers everything in the car. After thirty minutes, David approaches the Finnish border and crosses into safety.

David turns off the road near the Finnish border station and into a local gas station. His heart is pumping, and all his nerves are on edge. He knows he has taken a big risk traveling to Russia. He is despondent to be no closer to knowing what happened to his wife's remains.

He opens his tablet and launches an encrypted texting application. He proceeds to draft an encrypted email: *Dear George, I need your help. It has been a while since our last meeting in Moscow. Hope all is well. Can you set up a meeting between CIA HQ and myself? I am willing to meet in Finland. Thanks, David.* He sends the email and hopes he will be able to negotiate a deal with the CIA.

Chapter 34

Café CIA

Helsinki, Finland

On a cold autumn morning in Helsinki, David enters a café located in Kallio. He looks quite tense, as he is meeting with a CIA representative for the first time since he abandoned his post in Helsinki and traveled to Belarus to save Jaanika Olson. David is not sure what to expect from the United States government. He wonders if there is an outstanding arrest warrant issued for him by the United States authorities and whether they may attempt to arrest him.

David sits down at a small table in the back, orders a coffee, and nervously sits waiting. After ten minutes, a man in his twenties, whom he recognizes from his last meeting at the CIA headquarters, walks into the café wearing a trench coat, a suit, and a tie.

"David Markoff, I presume. I'm John Schroeder. I don't know if you recall, but we met at CIA headquarters." John shakes David's hand and presents a businesslike smile.

"Sit down," David remarks. He points to the chair across from him at the table. David feels quite tense due to John's approach.

"How was your trip to Finland?" David asks.

"Dark and dreary . . . like the weather. So, I finally meet the legend . . . the man who abandoned his post to save an American in Belarus and came back with great intelligence," John remarks. He pauses. "I have to be honest. If it were up to me, you would be kicked out of the CIA, prosecuted for dereliction of duty, and barred from entering CIA headquarters ever again," he adds.

"I am glad we are on such good terms and you hold me in such high esteem," David quips sarcastically and appears a little miffed. He pauses and takes a sip of coffee from a cup next to him. The tension between the two is quite palpable.

"Your name has reached the CIA director's office. It turns out the Finnish and Estonian governments have been pleading your case to the CIA director. The CIA's Counter-Intelligence Division also likes the fact that you uncovered Ambassador Armstrong's deceit and association with the Russian intelligence services. Consequently, I have traveled to Helsinki to offer you a reprieve and a promotion. You just have to sign a statement not to abandon your post again. In return, we will offer you a CIA posting at any place you desire," John says.

"I read on an Internet news site that Ambassador Armstrong has been allowed to resign quietly. Is that true?" David asks.

"I think they want to eliminate the possible damage to the president. He is a former high-ranking donor. You know Washington DC logic," John says. He flashes an expression indicating his disgust.

"I will swear not to abandon my post again. I want all that you have promised in writing, though, before I agree to your conditions," David says. David assesses that the best way to find the person who ordered his assassination and killed Terhi is to go back and work for the CIA again.

"Welcome back to the agency. I will get back to you," John remarks. He puts out his hand to shake. "Thanks." David smiles and firmly shakes John's hand.

David sits for a moment. He is startled by a tap on his shoulder and turns around and sees Greta, whom he last encountered at the United States embassy in Helsinki. She appears quite nervous. She is wearing a fur coat, a scarf, and glasses.

"Can we talk?" Greta asks. She surveys the café suspiciously.

"Uh . . . sure," David says. He grins and nonverbally motions for Greta to sit down with him in a chair opposite the table.

Greta proceeds to sit down. "It has been hard tracking you down. I have contacts in the SUPO and was able to track you down through them. I wanted to give you this file myself. You know that anything electronic is unsecure and can't be trusted," Greta says. She looks around the café to see if anyone could possibly be monitoring her conversation.

"Sure. Thanks for the warning before at the United States embassy. It saved my life. What do you need?" David says.

She takes out a folder from her knapsack and places the file next to David. "Here is your wife's file. I think it may solve an important mystery for you. I am providing this information to you in confidence and on behalf of a mutual friend. As far as I am concerned, this meeting never happened," Greta says.

"I don't know why you are helping me, but I really appreciate it. Thank you," David says.

"David, I am helping you as I am doing a favor for a friend yours that you have in Langley. Take care. I hope this helps you in some way. You realize this meeting never happened," Greta adds.

"Yes, I am aware of this. Again, thank you for your assistance. I don't know what to say." David smiles.

Greta rises from her chair and walks out of the café in haste.

David pauses for a moment, deep in thought. He looks around the café. He opens the file lying next to him. He flips the cover page and then sees a picture of Terhi. She looks quite young—no older than twenty-one. The report provides the name of Terhi as an aka and lists her true name as Tatiana Orlova Ivanova. David stares at her picture for a moment. He is stunned into disbelief, as he is overcome with emotions. Tears begin to roll down his face. He shakes a little for a moment and places his hands over his head. Then, he composes himself. He flips the page. The report states in Russian: *Tatiana is a Russian illegal sent by the Russian SVR and the Soviet KGB to obtain intelligence about the operations of the Finnish government.* It lists her date of birth and the fact that she was born in Leningrad, USSR. A chill goes down David's spine. His world is shaken. He wonders if the CIA knew about Terhi. *So many questions and so little answers. Nothing is ever what it seems in the intelligence world,* David thinks to himself. He looks around the café to see if anyone is watching him. He proceeds to take the file and place it inside his knapsack. David peers out the window of the café. He notices that white flakes of snow have begun to fall outside. David knows he will be back in Washington DC soon and realizes that he is lucky to have survived unscathed. He will return to the CIA headquarters as if nothing has happened since his departure. The short Nordic summer will seem to have been just a temporary illusion.

Epilogue

A Washington DC Debrief

David sits in a small white room located in the bowels of the CIA's Langley, Virginia headquarters with two stern-appearing individuals situated across the table. The air is tense, and the questions keep streaming as if no answer will stop their flow.

"How long were you traveling in Belarus?" the CIA investigator asks. He sits writing on his pad of paper.

"I told you this before. I was there only long enough to rescue my cousin and get her out of the country," David says. He crosses his arms and sits back in his chair.

"How exactly did you enter Belarus?" the investigator inquires again. He glances at the case file lying in front of him.

"As I stated during our last meeting, this was a spur-of-the-moment rescue operation. I used my unique skill set to enter and exit the country with false documents," David responds.

"Did you know your wife was a Russian illegal before the disappearance of her body?"

"No, actually. I thought she was a Finn. I was surprised to learn about her past and informed you when I discovered this fact." David sighs.

"OK, let's take a break. We may come back to these questions again," the investigator states.

"You know where I am located and my contact number if you have more questions," David says. He shakes his head in disgust.

David rises from his seat, walks from the small room located in the old office building, and proceeds to the lunchroom, which is situated in a beautiful cafeteria that possesses a skylight and a food court.

As David walks inside, he spots George, an old friend from Moscow, who is waiting in line for coffee at the small food court. David waves and approaches George.

"Nice to see you again. Are you based in Washington DC permanently now?" David asks.

"Yes. Let's sit down and talk for a minute," George says.

David escorts George to a small table that is set next to a small window in a corner of the lunchroom.

"David, I have to say that your escapades in Belarus are the talk of the Eastern European Bureau. Do you think the higher-ups trust you now?"

"I'm not sure. Do they really trust anyone very much in this building, especially a man from Vyborg, Russia?" David shakes his head in frustration. "Your stock can go up and then down. It all depends on events, luck, whom you know and who protects you, and your assignment. I feel like a survivor. I was not purged and am still employed by the agency. I even managed to save my cousin in the process. I would say I'm ahead of the game at this point," David says.

"When you think about it, that is the most you can hope for in Washington DC," George observes.

"Thanks for your support through all of this. I guess I can count on one person to back me up at the agency," David says.

"No thanks are needed. It is nice to help everyone. Where do you go from here?" George asks.

"I'm not sure. I am waiting on an assignment in Kiev, London, or Nairobi. The higher-ups promised me a prominent position, but the bureaucracy takes a long time," David says.

"Please keep in touch. I want to hear where you end up," George says.

David walks from the lunchroom to his parked car. He enters the car, starts the engine, proceeds to travel out of the CIA headquarters, and heads in the direction of Washington DC. He turns onto the Key Bridge and into Washington. He quickly proceeds up the northwestern section of the city and onto Wisconsin Avenue. He spots his destination and parks his car, which is situated next to the Russian embassy. The embassy possesses high gray walls and an imposing, drab façade. David walks up to a park that possesses a number of trees set on each corner of a walkway. The park is known as the Alley of Russian Poets. David looks around among the markers, each of which possesses a name of a famous Russian author written in Russian, including Aleksandr Pushkin, Mikhail Lermontov, and Fyodor Tyutchev. He approaches the main placard and places a flower next to it with an attached note written in Russian: *To my lost Russian love. You may be gone, but you will always be in my heart.*

He is silent for a moment. David instinctively feels that a burden has been lifted from his life, and his future—a location, identity, and mission yet unknown—awaits him.

CPSIA information can be obtained
at www.ICGtesting.com
Printed in the USA
LVOW13s1451200117
521663LV00009B/931/P